D1392761

'**What if I say I don't want anyone else, that I want you?**'

'Then you'll be in for a big disappointment.' Libby's breathing was rapid now. The way Warwick looked at her, a long, slow, calculated appraisal, was as intimate as if he were actually touching her, and to her shame she felt herself respond. She swung away, disgusted with herself. 'I have no intention of being treated as a plaything.'

CANARY ISLANDS

RELUCTANT HOSTAGE

BY

MARGARET MAYO

MILLS & BOON LIMITED
ETON HOUSE   18-24 PARADISE ROAD
RICHMOND   SURREY   TW9 1SR

For Tina and Andy
Happy memories always

All the characters in this book have no existence outside the imagination of the Author, and have no relation whatsoever to anyone bearing the same name or names. They are not even distantly inspired by any individual known or unknown to the Author, and all the incidents are pure invention.

All Rights Reserved. The text of this publication or any part thereof may not be reproduced or transmitted in any form or by any means, electronic or mechanical, including photocopying, recording, storage in an information retrieval system, or otherwise, without the written permission of the publisher.

This book is sold subject to the condition that it shall not, by way of trade or otherwise, be lent, resold, hired out or otherwise circulated without the prior consent of the publisher in any form of binding or cover other than that in which it is published and without a similar condition including this condition being imposed on the subsequent purchaser.

First published in Great Britain 1992
by Mills & Boon Limited

© Margaret Mayo 1992

Australian copyright 1992
Philippine copyright 1992
This edition 1992

ISBN 0 263 77540 2

Set in Times Roman 10 on 11½ pt.
01-9205-55269 C

Made and printed in Great Britain

CHAPTER ONE

THE man's smoky eyes were still on her, not wavering to left or right, making Libby feel that she was the centre of his universe, that no one and nothing else mattered. It was a whole new experience. The unaccustomed warmth that had started in the pit of her stomach had spread to every corner of her body. It was a feeling that surpassed all other feelings, creating exciting, alien sensations. And the fact that it was happening to her, plain Libby Eaton, whom boys rarely looked at twice, made it all the more amazing.

'I think we should introduce ourselves. My name's Warwick.' His smile was easy and all-consuming, and Libby felt as though she were drowning in the depths of his eyes, which was madness, insanity, but she hadn't the will-power to shake him off, to snap out of this plethora of feelings and emotions that had surprisingly crept over her.

He held out his hand as he spoke, and hesitantly she took it. It was the first physical contact they had made since the plane had left Heathrow more than three hours earlier, and tiny shock waves of electricity stabbed through her, heightening the feelings that already existed. His hand was warm and strong and held hers in a grip so firm that it told her this chance meeting meant something to him too.

'Libby,' she announced shyly, her response coming a mere second after his question, yet it felt like an aeon.

'Libby?' He gave her name a whole new meaning, making it sound special and somehow sexy. She had never heard it said in quite the same way. He had a deep voice with an unusual timbre that sent shivers of pleasure down her spine. 'Is that short for anything?'

'Elizabeth, but I'm never called that.'

'I prefer Libby too. It suits you. You're not an Elizabeth. Libby suggests a softer, more feminine person. Mmm, yes, Libby; I like it.' Still he held her hand, and Libby's whole body felt as if it were on fire.

'And how old are you, little girl with the beautiful name?'

'Little girl'? She was five feet seven! And as for feminine, well, Rebecca was the glamour girl, the pretty one, the one who was never short of boyfriends. Libby had always considered herself unattractive and gauche. 'I'm twenty-three,' she announced, almost defiantly.

A thick dark brow rose. 'So old!' he mocked.

'And you, what are you? Twenty-eight, twenty-nine?'

'Thirty-four.'

'So old!' she returned, laughing, but it was old to her. The only boys she had felt any interest in had been nearer her own age.

Finally he let go of her hand, and Libby was left with the sensation of a million electric impulses shooting through her skin. She clasped her two hands together and savoured the feeling. This was a moment in life to be remembered. It was doubtful she would see this man again once they touched down in Tenerife. He was a ship that passed in the night, a magical stranger who made her feel like a different girl.

Libby's experience of men was limited. She was too conscious of the fact that she was a mere pale shadow of her beautiful sister, too uninteresting to hold the attention of any man for long. Besides, there had been little time for boyfriends since their mother died. When she wasn't working there was always so much to do in the house.

'Are you married?' The question was out before she could stop it and her cheeks coloured with faint embarrassment. But it troubled her to think he could be expertly playing with her emotions. She wanted to savour the memory with no regrets.

'Would it bother you if I were?'

Libby did not know how to answer that. To say yes would reveal too much, but to say no would be a lie. She lifted her narrow shoulders in what she hoped was a careless shrug. 'It was idle curiosity.'

He grinned, not believing her for one second. 'No, I'm not married, Libby.'

'Do you live in Tenerife?' Although they had talked non-stop for most of the journey, it had been nonsense talk: anecdotes, observations, ambitions. He had told her that he wanted to fly to the moon, she had said she wanted to own an island. It was obvious from his accent that he was English, but that was all she knew.

He nodded. 'I have done for the last twelve years.'

'Do you intend spending the rest of your life there?'

It was his turn to shrug. 'I might do. I've really no long-term plans at the moment.'

'What do you do for a living?'

He laughed. 'All these questions. It is of no consequence at this moment what I do. Today you are the most important person in my life. You have transformed a mundane flight into something magical. I have made this trip dozens of times, but never met a girl who has made me forget the tedium of repetition.'

Could he really be talking about her? thought Libby. Her straight ash-blonde hair was too pale and thin to be attractive, unlike her sister's thick golden locks that hung over her shoulders in a tumult of rich waves. Her complexion was too pale as well, and her wide eyes made her look like a waif.

And yet the way this man spoke, the way he looked at her, made her feel different, almost beautiful. It was a foreign and totally unexpected sensation, and goose-bumps rose on her skin as he continued to appraise her.

'I'm not a seasoned traveller myself,' she admitted. 'In fact flying makes me nervous.' She had only ever flown once before, and that was on a short holiday to Jersey when their parents were alive. Yet now, with this man at her side, she had not given it a thought. From the moment she'd sat down she had been aware of nothing but him.

'You've not shown your fear today.'

That's because of you, she wanted to say, but he knew it anyway. It was there in the way he looked at her. He had such deep-seeing eyes, an unusual blue-grey, with thick dark lashes. His hair was almost black, cut quite short and brushed back, only the front few strands falling untidily and yet attractively forward. His deeply tanned skin covered the chiselled bones of his face. There was a raw masculinity about him that could not be ignored.

A nice face, she thought, kind and considerate. He had a full lower lip, suggesting he might be a passionate lover, and Libby felt her skin crawl again. Why was she thinking like this? What madness was possessing her? She had never entertained such thoughts in her life.

'Are you cold?' His hand came over hers again, a frown of concern in his eyes.

'Someone walking over my grave.' She tried to laugh off the feeling, but it was a poor attempt—a weak smile, no more, as her eyes were drawn to his.

It happened now as it had earlier—everyone else on the plane became non-existent. They were in their own private universe where hearts thudded and pulses raced—

and, as there was no likelihood of this chance meeting developing into any sort of relationship, she decided she might as well make the most of it—and then forget him!

Libby's eyes, which she disparagingly called mauve, and privately thought were too large for her face, were an unusual amethyst. Unknown to herself, they were sometimes a deep, regal purple, sometimes as pale as lavender blossom. At this moment, as hunger for this man took possession of her, they were richly purple, full and luminous, seeking and searching every plane of his face, every pore, every line.

He let her hand go, and she felt strangely bereft, and at that moment the captain announced that they would soon be approaching Tenerife's Reina Sofia airport. Sadness welled up inside Libby, a deep, unremitting sadness that threatened to fill every corner of her being. The end of a beautiful, unexpected encounter was near, and she did not want it to happen. She wanted this flight to go on for ever.

Briefly she looked at Warwick, and he saw the sadness and smiled. 'I hope this isn't going to be the end, Libby. I shall see you again?'

This was something she had not expected, and she looked at him with wide, surprised eyes. She really had thought this was a brief passage in time, that he would say goodbye and that would be that. She wanted to see him again, yes, of course she did, but she did not want him meeting her sister—she did not want to run the risk of losing him to someone who was far more attractive than she.

It went without saying that once he met Rebecca it would be all over. It was a fact of life. No matter how much he might think he liked her now, once he met her beautiful younger sister . . .

'I'm not sure it will be possible,' she said huskily, hurting inside as she uttered the words. 'I intend spending all of my time with my sister. This is actually a surprise visit—I haven't seen her for months. We have a lot to catch up on.' She had already told him that she was paying Rebecca a visit.

'That's a pity.' He made no attempt to hide his disappointment. 'I was hoping to see more of you.' His hand on her arm paralysed her—not firm, the lightest touch, but holding her in its power as though it were a vice. 'Perhaps I'll be able to persuade you to change your mind?'

'I don't think so.' Libby felt a sense of impending deprivation as she uttered the words. She could not understand how or why she felt so strongly when she had known him for only a few hours, but she would far rather lose Warwick now and save the happy memories than risk losing him to Rebecca. Rebecca was a vulture where men were concerned.

He moved his hand and looked away through the window. Libby became aware of the girl sitting in the seat next to her. It was hard to believe that she had not known of her existence. She smiled at her faintly, and wondered if the girl had heard all that had been going on, whether she was an interested observer, and would be telling her friends. Then Warwick spoke again, and the girl was forgotten.

'You'll like Tenerife; it's an island of contrasts—both in lifestyle and geographically. Do you like discos and plenty of night-life? Or is a quiet dinner and a stroll along the beach more your scene?'

Libby had not been to many discos—not from personal choice but because of circumstances at home. 'A bit of each, I suppose,' she said, adding, 'It all depends on the mood I'm in.'

'And the person you're with?'

She did not miss the meaning behind his words. 'The person I'm with,' she agreed—not that she had ever gone out with a man where they'd done anything so romantic as walking along a beach when it was dark. The very infrequent dates she'd had were to the cinema or the local pub in the East End of London where she lived, and a quick peck on the cheek at the end of the evening was all any of them had managed. It had done nothing for her self-esteem, confirming only what she already knew: that she wasn't attractive to any man—*until now*! She still couldn't get over it.

'I prefer a quiet life myself. Good food, good wine and good company. Not for me the bright lights. I had enough of that in my youth.'

Libby smiled. 'You make me sound young and yourself old.'

'Ten years is sometimes a lifetime. On the other hand it can pass in an instant.'

Libby knew what he meant, but it would need a unique relationship to make life go that quickly. *Such as could develop between themselves!* Was that what he was suggesting? After a mere four hours? It sounded crazy, and yet Libby felt the same deep gut reaction that had drawn him to her.

Their attention was diverted by the hostess requesting passengers to make sure their seatbelts were fastened and to extinguish all cigarettes. Libby lapsed into an unhappy silence as the plane made its final descent. Was she doing the wrong thing in saying that she did not want to see him again? Perhaps he wouldn't fancy Rebecca. Perhaps she was being overly cautious.

Her thoughts tailed away as the plane landed and they waited their turn to get off. The heat hit her like a blast from an oven as they descended the steps, and as they waited for their luggage in the grey concrete building she was vitally conscious of Warwick still at her side. He was much taller than she had imagined, standing a good eight inches above her.

Their cases retrieved, he accompanied her outside to the line of waiting taxis. It was already growing dark. 'Perhaps we can share?' he suggested, making it clear that he was as anxious as she to prolong their time together. 'Where is your sister staying?'

'Torviscas—but I'm sure it must be out of your way.' Rebecca had told her that it was on the outskirts of Playa de las Américas, the popular tourist area. He would surely live nowhere close to that?

'Not at all,' he said with an encouraging smile. 'By a strange coincidence that's precisely my own destination. Something tells me, Libby, that you're not going to escape from me as easily as you think.'

She felt flattered and enormously pleased, but suddenly apprehensive also. She really did not want him to meet Rebecca. In the taxi, thigh touching thigh, his hand on hers, adrenalin pumping and pulses racing, she wondered again if she was over-reacting.

'Do you realise I don't even know your second name?' he said.

'Nor do I know yours,' she rejoined with a soft smile.

'Hunter,' he supplied readily.

'Eaton,' she grimaced. 'I've never liked it.'

'Eaton? Your sister wouldn't be named Rebecca by any chance?'

Libby nodded. 'That's right, and she works on a ship called the *Estoque*. Do you know it?'

'By another quirk of fate, Libby, yes, I do. The *Estoque* belongs to me.'

Libby was astounded at the coincidence, and felt a moment's panic as she wondered if he was already involved with Rebecca. But there was nothing at all in his expression to suggest her sister meant anything to him. His smile was as warm and encompassing as it had ever been.

A broad smile broke out on her face. She was worrying for nothing. Warwick wouldn't have paid her so much attention if he had been attracted to Rebecca. Everything was suddenly wonderful. 'I can't believe it!' she said excitedly. 'What a small world it is.'

'A small world indeed,' he agreed. 'It looks as though we're going to see a lot more of each other than you thought.'

Libby was so estatically happy that she did not notice the hardness that had entered his eyes, or the sudden tension in his body.

The journey took no more than twenty minutes along a good fast road, but by the time they got there it was completely dark. No long-drawn-out dusks here; once the sun went down it was dark within minutes.

Puerto Colon was a man-made marina, flanked by bars and boutiques, restaurants and palm trees. Ships were anchored in regimented rows, and the whole scene was floodlit. The water looked bottle-green in the artificial light and the wind slapped ropes against masts in a musical melody. People strolled and watched and laughed, and Warwick led her along a pontoon to a boat which was the last in a line.

The *Estoque* was large and imposing, painted white or some other pale colour—it was difficult to tell in the electric light. Inside was a huge saloon where the steering-wheel, radar screen and a host of other very impressive-looking equipment occupied one corner. There was velvet seating in a relaxing dove-grey, a deep-piled ruby carpet, a table, a bookcase, a drinks cabinet. It wanted for nothing. But there was no Rebecca!

'Your sister is out most evenings,' Warwick said unconcernedly. 'It's too early yet for her to be back. Do sit down. Can I get you something to eat, or a drink perhaps, while you're waiting?'

'No, thank you,' Libby answered quietly. She felt shy of this man on his home ground, an inexplicable shyness that was at odds with the feelings she had entertained earlier. Perhaps it was because they had been cocooned together on the plane, so that there was no escaping him? The intimacy enforced. Now, with space between them, she could think rationally.

He sat opposite, looking at her with a quizzical expression in his eyes. 'You look nothing like your sister.'

Libby gave an inward groan. Here it came—the disparaging comparison she had been used to all her life.

'Rebecca's beauty is superficial, yours comes from deep down inside.'

Beautiful? He was saying she was beautiful?

'You have an inner serenity that reflects itself in your demeanour and your lovely eyes. You're quite right to wear very little make-up; you don't need it. Your sister slaps it on like layers of paint. It's enough to put any man off.' Libby's heart beat uncomfortably fast at these compliments. 'You're a lovely young woman, Libby. I find it difficult to believe that you're related to Rebecca. Yes, very difficult; there's no comparison between you. What are your parents like? Whom do you take after?'

Libby shrugged, his flattery, the soft expression in his eyes creating havoc with her senses. Simply looking at him, listening to his deep, sexy voice was enough to melt her bones, and she knew that if she got up she would be unable to stand. It was a whole new experience.

'My mother had the same pale complexion as me, though her hair was golden like Rebecca's.'

'Is your mother no longer alive?' he asked softly, noting her use of the past tense.

'She died three years ago.' Libby's face clouded at the painful memory. Alcoholic poisoning, the doctor had said; Libby preferred to think it was a broken heart.

'I'm sorry,' he said compassionately. 'And your father?'

She compressed her lips, wishing he weren't asking all these questions. 'He's dead too. Nearly eight years ago he had a fatal accident at work. My mother never got over it.'

Libby would never forget the day her mother had been brought the news of Jim Eaton's death. A freak accident, they'd told her, a one-in-a-million chance. Mary Eaton had collapsed, and was inconsolable; she did not want to live without him, and over the years she had turned more and more to the bottle for comfort, leaving the running of the house to Libby.

Rebecca had been ten when her father died, wayward even then, becoming even more uncontrollable without his firm supervision, and, with the death of her mother when she was almost sixteen, she would listen to nothing Libby ever said. 'I'm grown-up now,' she'd declared haughtily. 'Who are you to tell me what to do?' She'd only ever turned to Libby when she was short of money.

Once the police had called at the house, saying that Rebecca had taken part in a robbery from one of the local big houses. Libby had nearly gone out of her mind with worry until it had transpired that Rebecca had not been involved at all—that a girl with a grudge against her because Rebecca had stolen her boyfriend had deliberately tried to get her into trouble. Fortunately Rebecca had an excellent alibi, but it had nevertheless been a worrying time for Libby.

She was fortunate that in her job as a self-employed, mobile hairdresser, either going out to clients' homes in her battered Mini, or using their own front room as a salon, she had been able to spend a lot of time looking after her mother, and always tried to be at home when Rebecca came out of school. Every penny she'd earned had gone into the house—or to Rebecca!

'So you two girls were left alone? What sort of an upbringing did you have? Were your parents strong on discipline?'

Libby shot him a sharp glance at this unexpected question, feeling sure it had something to do with Rebecca. Or was she being too sensitive? 'My father was, yes,' she admitted. 'He was very old-fashioned in his attitudes. My mother wasn't so bad, but once he died she had no interest in anything. She was broken-hearted. It was left to me to bring up my sister. Do you think she'll be long?'

'I'm sure not,' he said reassuringly, and, after a moment's pause, 'I see now why you're so different. Rebecca would appear to take after your father. She has very strong convictions, and probably rebelled over what she saw as his totally outmoded views, whereas you are as soft and sensitive as your mother, and, although you did your best after she died, Rebecca went very much her own way.'

He was so uncannily accurate that Libby wondered whether Rebecca had told him about their home circumstances.

'No, your sister hasn't said anything,' he assured her, almost as though she had asked the question out aloud. 'Please, let me pour you a drink.' Without more ado he walked across to the drinks cabinet. 'Gin? Campari? Bacardi?'

'Just a tonic water, please,' she said. Unaccustomed to alcohol, she feared it might go to her head. It was all very well feeling attracted to him on the plane, where there had been safety in numbers, but here, with just the two of them, she could find herself in an uncomfortable situation. And she was still stunned by his summing up. Was he able to judge all people so accurately?

He looked surprised by her choice, but nevertheless filled a glass with ice and a slice of lemon and poured the tonic over it. With a flourish he presented it to her. 'For you, *señorita*, one very special drink.'

Libby took it from him with a smile, feeling the power that emanated from him to her as their fingers touched. He seemed in no hurry to move away. 'Aren't you drinking anything?' she asked, surprised to hear how breathless she sounded.

'But of course.' He turned and poured a generous measure of whisky into a glass and then resumed the seat he had been sitting in earlier.

As the minutes passed Libby began to get more and more restless, constantly looking at her watch. It was almost midnight now, and still no sign of Rebecca.

'Don't worry,' he said, 'your sister is a night-bird.'

'What if she doesn't come back?' she asked worriedly. 'What if she stays out all night? Has she ever done that?' Frequently at home Rebecca had stayed with friends, but she had always rung Libby to tell her where she was— persuaded, Libby suspected, by her friend's parents, but at least she had never needed to worry as to her whereabouts. Here she could be anywhere and doing heaven knew what. Into the drug scene, anything. It didn't bear thinking about.

'Rebecca has always been here to cook my meals,' he told her, which was no answer at all.

This was something else that had bothered Libby when Rebecca had written and told her that she had got a job as a cook and deck-hand on a cabin cruiser. Rebecca, cooking? It didn't sound right; it was far too domesticated for her fun-loving sister. Her initial thoughts were that there was a man involved, but, having met Warwick, having heard him say that her sister was not his type, she knew this was not the case. So why was her sister working here, doing jobs she had always abhorred at home?

When Rebecca had announced six months ago that England had nothing to offer and she was going out to the Canary Islands to look for work, Libby had nearly had a fit. It was Rebecca's own fault that she was unemployable, she'd told her. 'If you'd worked harder at school you'd have had some qualifications. What do you think you're going to do out there?' But Rebecca had not listened and, together with Zelda Sanders, a friend from her school days, she had packed her bags and gone.

Zelda's elder brother, Mark, was working out there selling timeshares, and he'd said he could get them a job too. From what Libby had gathered it hadn't exactly worked out like that. They'd lived together in his cramped quarters for a while, but Rebecca had been unable to find work, and when Mark had lost his job and couldn't afford the apartment Rebecca had been desperate until she'd landed this job with Warwick Hunter.

'But what if she doesn't turn up until early in the morning? What am I going to do?'

'Sleep here,' he told her simply. 'You can use Rebecca's cabin.'

But Libby, for all that this man aroused the most sensual feelings in her body, had no wish to sleep alone on the boat with him. He was still an unknown quantity, and, although he seemed like a gentleman, who could say whether his intentions were honourable?

'I—I don't think that would be a very good idea,' she said. 'I'll go and find a hotel, and come back in the morning.' When she'd decided to come out here her plans had been very vague. She had hoped there would be room on the boat where Rebecca worked for her to stay too, but she hadn't banked on it, and had enough money with her to stay in a hotel if necessary—but only a very cheap one.

As she stood up she missed his frown of faint annoyance. 'You don't have to do this, Libby,' he said, rising too, the frown gone now, the warm smile she had grown used to back in place.

His touch on her arm was electric. 'I really would prefer it,' she murmured huskily. 'Perhaps you can recommend somewhere?'

The hotel was but a few minutes' walk away from Puerto Colon. Warwick insisted on accompanying her, and she was glad of his assistance when she discovered that the night porter spoke only Spanish. In fact she was impressed by Warwick's fluency in the language.

A room was found for her, and Warwick carried up her case, waving away offers of help. At her door he said, 'You can still change your mind, Libby. You're welcome to sleep on board my boat.'

His eyes looked deeply into hers, stirring her soul, making it almost impossible to refuse. But common sense asserted itself, and she shook her head. 'Do you really think I'd be able to sleep?'

He grinned. 'Maybe you're right.'

'And I'll be back first thing in the morning.'

She was disappointed when he did not kiss her, when he merely took her hands and again looked at her with an intentness that set every nerve-end twitching and every pulse stammering. 'Until tomorrow, then, my beautiful Libby.'

'Tomorrow,' she agreed with a faint whisper.

Warwick Hunter really was an extraordinary man—so different from anyone else she had ever met. His age had a lot to do with it, she supposed. He was far more sophisticated, more assured, more experienced. Yes, experienced. He knew how to look at a woman and have her melting without a word being spoken. He had mastered the art of flattery, and could probably bend any woman to his will.

So was she making a fool of herself? Did it mean nothing more to him than a casual flirtation? Libby did not like to think so. She had sensed a sincerity in him that was certainly not false. There had definitely been a strong chemical reaction between them, but something deeper too. It was not easy for her to decide what it was, but it went far beyond basic needs.

Although it was late when she went to bed Libby was still awake at seven, and, after a shower and a light breakfast of croissants and coffee, she made her way towards the marina.

Not many people were about at this hour, and she wondered if she was too soon, whether the boat would be locked and silent, its inhabitants still fast asleep. But, when she looked across at the *Estoque*, the man who had made such a big impression on her was standing on the deck—almost as though he was watching and waiting for *her*!

She hastened her steps, but the hurried beats of her heart took her by surprise. It was not a feeling she was used to. How could she feel so disturbed simply by looking at a man from this distance? What sort of power was it that he wielded over her?

She wore jeans this morning and trainers, and a thin T-shirt, because despite the time of day it was already very warm. She had dripped with perspiration during the night, as there was no air-conditioning in the room, and taken another shower this morning, but already again she was uncomfortably hot. Her hair was tied back in a pony-tail and she had not bothered with make-up. For one thing she had been in too much of a rush, for another she remembered Warwick's words that he hated too much of it. If he liked her as she was, then she had no need to try and impress him.

He took her hand and helped her on board, and her body reacted instantly to his touch; but her first words were about Rebecca. She had had time to think during the night, to realise that she had been in danger of letting Warwick fill her mind to the exclusion of all else. Rebecca was the reason she was here; she must never lose sight of that.

He led her down into the saloon before answering, pouring her a cup of coffee from the pot that was keeping warm in the galley. 'Milk and sugar?'

'Just milk, please,' she said impatiently. 'Rebecca? Where is she? Is she still asleep?'

'I'm afraid she never came back.'

'Never came back?' Libby felt the colour drain out of her face. 'But that's impossible; she must be here. Where is she if she's not? Warwick, something must have happened to her!'

CHAPTER TWO

'I'M sure there's some perfectly good explanation,'
Warwick told Libby succinctly. 'It was a pity you didn't
let your sister know you were coming out here. Surprises
are all very well, but they can fall flat.'

'Does she often stay out all night?' Libby reminded
him of her previously unanswered question.

'I'm not Rebecca's keeper, Libby. I'm merely her employer. And surely she's at an age where she is free to
do what she likes?'

'She's only eighteen.'

His brows lifted. 'I thought she was older.'

'She gives that impression,' Libby rejoined drily. 'You
claim she's always here to cook your breakfast. What
time is that?'

'About eight.'

'And it's almost that now,' claimed Libby, glancing
at her wristwatch. 'She's cutting it a bit fine, don't you
think?'

'If for some reason she's detained, she'll send a
message, I'm sure,' he said quietly, but as the minutes
ticked away they heard nothing, and as morning pro-
gressed into afternoon Libby began to get seriously
worried.

'I think we ought to contact the police,' she said.

'And what would we tell them?' he asked reasonably.
'It's too soon, Libby. She'll either turn up or be in touch.
Whatever is detaining her must be out of her control.'

'Was she happy working for you?' asked Libby
sharply. She felt so responsible for her sister. She hadn't

22

been keen on her leaving home in the first place. What if she'd got in with the wrong crowd? Who knew where she was or what she was doing? 'Cooking and cleaning isn't exactly the sort of thing Rebecca enjoys.'

His lips suddenly quirked. 'For the first few days I thought I was being poisoned, but she learned quickly when I made her eat her own food. Yes, I would say she's happy here. She certainly never complains.'

The thought of Warwick and Rebecca sitting and eating together disturbed Libby. It wasn't the sort of relationship she had expected them to have. Had anything else happened between them? Was there something she did not know? 'So why did you employ her in the first place?' she asked with some asperity.

'She was introduced by an acquaintance of mine,' he told her. 'He said she desperately needed a job with accommodation thrown in. Like a fool, I thought all women could cook. Nevertheless she pulled her weight, did whatever I asked of her, and was appropriately decorative about the place.'

Libby imagined this last was at least accurate. She could imagine Rebecca sunbathing in a minuscule bikini on the deck. Rebecca coming out of the shower with nothing but a towel between her and her modesty. Rebecca in all sorts of seductive poses. That was the sort of girl her sister was. But where was she now? And why wasn't Warwick as worried as she?

'Are you sure you don't know where she is?' she asked in sudden suspicion.

'You think I wouldn't tell you if I did?' His tone was surprisingly sharp. 'I'm as anxious to find your sister as you are.'

'But not anxious to involve the police?' she swiftly returned.

'Simply because it's too soon,' he pointed out.

'Can I have a look at my sister's room?' He was right, but what else could they do? How long did he expect her to wait before they did anything?

'Of course; it's down here.' A short flight of steps led through the galley and dinette, a cursory glance revealing an inset microwave oven and refrigerator, everywhere spotlessly clean. Between the galley and dining area a door led into the forecabin, which was much larger than she had expected, with a double bed and plenty of hanging space and cupboards, and behind another door was a shower-room.

Libby looked into the wardrobe, and was surprised by the number of new dresses Rebecca had bought in the short time she'd been working for Warwick. He either paid her very well or... The alternative did not bear thinking about.

'It doesn't look as though she was planning not to come back,' commented Warwick. He was standing close behind her, his hands on her shoulders, his breath warm on her cheek. Libby felt her senses tingle, but concern for her sister had to take precedence.

She pulled away from him. 'I still think there is something terribly wrong.'

He shrugged. 'If it will make you happy I'll go and have a word with the *policía*, even though I think it's premature. Your sister has always given the impression that she's more than capable of looking after herself.'

'But she wouldn't just disappear without leaving word,' Libby insisted. 'Rebecca might have her faults, but she wouldn't do that. There is something wrong, I know there is.'

She hurried up the steps to the saloon, but when she would have left the boat Warwick put a detaining hand on her arm. 'I'll go alone. You wouldn't want to miss Rebecca if she turns up, would you?'

'Of course not.'

'I won't be long,' he promised, holding her hands and looking deeply into her eyes.

Libby felt herself quiver. They were still all there—the feelings she had felt so strongly on the plane, and once Rebecca was found, once she knew her sister was safe, then they could take up where they had left off. She gave him a wan smile. 'I'm sorry,' she whispered.

'It's not your fault,' he replied and, lifting her hands, he placed a kiss, gently, in each palm. 'I'll be as quick as I can.'

When he had gone Libby paced the saloon anxiously, then, because it was so stiflingly hot, she made her way out on to the deck and sat in the sunshine, her hands clasped around her knees, absently watching holiday-makers strolling by, but not really taking in the busy scene.

When she tired of sitting she pushed herself to her feet and took a walk around the marina. It was filled with boats of all sorts: yachts, motor cruisers such as the *Estoque*—some larger, some smaller—catamarans, speed-boats. It was a fascinating sight. Most of them were silent and empty, but some were a hive of activity, decks being hosed, paintwork touched up; one was slowly making its way out of the mouth of the harbour and another was getting ready to leave.

She strolled around and climbed some steps up on to the harbour wall, where she had an uninterrupted view across the Atlantic Ocean. Here the breeze lifted her hair and cooled her skin, but never did she let the *Estoque* out of her sight. When she saw Warwick return she quickly joined him.

'Well, what did they say?' she asked at once.

He grimaced. 'As I said, it's too soon for them to do anything. A few hours is nothing. A few days might be more serious.'

' "A few days"?' asked Libby in alarm. 'This is preposterous. I can't just sit and wait, it's out of the question.'

'I'm afraid that's all we can do.' His hand was comforting on her arm, his voice soft and reassuring.

She felt a feathering along her nerves, and again wondered how she could feel such sensations when Rebecca was missing. It seemed that this man had the ability to make her forget everything except him.

'You must be hungry,' he said, breaking into her thoughts. 'How about if I cook us a meal?'

'I couldn't eat,' confessed Libby. The very thought of food made her feel ill.

'You need to keep up your strength,' he told her firmly. 'I'll make us something you'll find impossible to resist.'

Libby knew it would be pointless to protest, and to be truthful it felt good to let him take over. She sat down again and closed her eyes, letting the late afternoon sun wash over her, and the next thing she knew Warwick was touching her arm and telling her to wake up.

For a few seconds Libby did not know where she was. She felt warm and lethargic, and Warwick's face close to hers made her heartbeats quicken. She wanted to pull him down beside her, to draw her strength from him, to savour once again all the new and wonderful sensations she had experienced on the plane.

She had no idea how appealing she looked, her amethyst eyes soft and misted from sleep, her cheeks flushed, her ash-blonde hair attractively tousled. She took his extended hand and let him help her up, and the next second found herself pulled against a chest that was packed with hard muscle.

'My lovely Libby, you're irresistible,' he muttered against her ear.

Her heart hammered with all the intensity of a jungle drum; in fact it was so painful she could feel it right up into her throat. She let herself savour for a moment the unusual experience of having a man such as Warwick Hunter find her desirable.

With one hand still behind her back his other moved up to touch her throat, to feel the shape of her chin and the softness of her lips. Libby felt she was drowning in a thousand different sensations. He kissed the tip of her *retroussé* nose, each cheek, her eyelids, her brow, her ears. Her lips parted as she hungrily waited for him to claim her mouth. For the moment all thoughts of Rebecca had fled.

His kiss was a long time in coming. He touched her lips again with gentle, exploratory fingers, almost like a blind man trying to familiarise himself with the shape of her wide mouth. Involuntarily she ran the tip of her tongue over suddenly dry lips, feeling a spasm of pleasure pulse through her as she accidentally touched the abrasive roughness of his fingertip.

When he pulled down her lower lip and kissed the warm, soft moistness inside she squirmed with unexpected pleasure, surprised to hear a whimper, an animal sound almost, escape the back of her throat. Without even kissing her properly he was arousing her more than all the other boys she had dated put together.

He feathered her lips with tiny kisses, traced the outline with his tongue, creating a new flurry of excitement so that she felt as if her bones were melting, and if he let her go she would sink into a heap on the floor and disappear like a snowball in the sunshine.

Without her even realising it, her arms had snaked behind him, and beneath her palms she felt the ripple of powerful muscle. She had an insane urge to work her hands up beneath his shirt and explore the exciting warmth of his bare skin. She had never, in the whole of her life, felt like this. It was a wanton, primeval feeling that both shocked and thrilled her, but, when her hips ground instinctively against his, when she discovered that he was equally excited, she pulled abruptly away, daunted by the thought that she had been able to do this to him.

He smiled, a gentle smile that suggested he understood, though Libby knew he didn't. How could he know that for her age she was very naïve? That looking after her mother and Rebecca had left her little time for personal relationships? Or the fact that because she was the ugly sister she had been reluctant to go out anyway? It all added up to the fact that she knew nothing at all about men, and was scared now of the situation in which she found herself.

'Let's eat,' he said, tucking her arm through his, and leading the way back inside.

An unexpected sight met her eyes. Fresh bread, sliced thinly and made into salmon and cucumber sandwiches, fruit cake, strawberries and cream. A pot of tea and china cups. So typically English that she was stunned. She had thought he would cook a proper meal, something Spanish, something which, in her present agitated condition, would be completely indigestible.

His eyes looked wickedly amused. 'You look surprised.'

'I am,' she confessed.

'I thought you needed something to tempt your taste-buds. Do sit down.'

Libby astonished herself by eating hungrily. The bread was crusty and fresh, spread with butter and plenty of salmon. It was the most appetising meal she had eaten in a long time. The fresh strawberries, too, were sweet and juicy, and by the time she had finished she felt somehow happier. Pleasantly replete, and with a man looking at her as though she were a princess, what more could she want?

After they had finished eating they moved into the saloon, Warwick surprising her by sitting a distance away. Even so his eyes were constantly on her, keeping the flame alight that he had ignited earlier, making her wish that the world were theirs alone, that there were no external worries to take her mind away from him.

But of course there was Rebecca—Rebecca her recalcitrant sister who was disturbingly missing. It was dark again now; another day had passed, and still there was no sign of her.

'Worrying about your sister won't do you any good,' said Warwick.

Libby pulled a wry face. 'How can I help it? She came out here with a friend, Zelda Sanders. Perhaps she might know where Rebecca is, or even her brother Mark? They lived together for a while—until he lost his job and couldn't afford the apartment. I think that's when Rebecca came to you. There's also the man who asked you if you'd find her a job. He might know. I'm sure there are lots of things we could be doing?'

'I've already contacted the guy who introduced Rebecca; he knows nothing,' he told her. 'And, as for friends, she never mentioned names or brought anyone here. I have no idea where this Zelda or Mark might be living. There really is very little more we can do for the moment.'

'But I feel so helpless,' Libby protested. 'We must do something. People don't go missing for no reason.'

Warwick put his hands to her shoulders and looked at her in concern. 'Libby, if you're going to go out of your mind worrying, I don't think it would be a good idea staying in your hotel room alone. I think you should sleep here.'

Her eyes widened, beautiful amethyst orbs in a face that was prettily flushed with the warmth of the afternoon's sun. Her pulses quickened as she remembered his suffocating closeness on the deck earlier, and her whole body went on instant alert.

'You'll be quite safe, I assure you.' Again he knew exactly what she was thinking.

How could he say that when he had given proof of how much he desired her? But hadn't she been equally guilty? And, apart from the lightest of kisses, had he made any demands on her body? Of course he hadn't. In fact he had been far more of a gentleman than she'd expected, and he was right—she would worry about Rebecca. She wanted to be here the second her sister came back, not stuck in a hotel room where she would know nothing until morning. But it was still a risky thing to do, and her mind warred with itself as she struggled to make a decision.

'Libby,' he said softly, 'there's a lock on Rebecca's door. I simply thought it would be the best solution—for you, not me.'

She nodded, her lips compressed, her face wry. 'You're right, of course. I'd worry like anything away from here; I probably wouldn't even sleep.'

'Whereas you'll be able to sleep like a baby, confident in the knowledge that when Rebecca returns you'll be woken instantly.'

'I've never done anything like this before,' she muttered uneasily.

'Your sister's never gone absent before,' he reminded her. 'I think you owe it to her, if not to yourself, to be here.'

'You're confident that she'll come back?'

'Most definitely. She wouldn't have left any of her dresses if she'd planned on moving out. I've learned enough about Rebecca to know how much she loves clothes. She's probably gone to one of those parties that go on for days on end. She'll turn up.'

'Not a drugs party?' asked Libby in horror.

'Of course not. Rebecca's far too sensible. I've never known a girl with such a level head on her shoulders— for her age. That's why I thought she was so much older.'

He was taking it all remarkably calmly, Libby thought, as though people often went missing for a couple of days. But it wasn't his sister who was involved; he couldn't really have any idea how upset she was.

'I'll stay,' she said softly, mentally crossing her fingers that she was making the right decision. On the other hand did it matter if they became lovers? *Lovers?* Even the word sounded exciting. That indefinable something that had brought them together on the plane was not a figment of her imagination, she was sure. They had both felt it, were both aware that it was something special and rare and magical. Many people went through their whole life without experiencing anything like it. And who was she to be so expert on this sort of thing? She was deluding herself; this wasn't the way of things at all.

'I'm sure you won't regret it, Libby.' Warwick's tone was low and persuasive. 'I knew on the plane that our meeting was predestined.' Libby smiled, relieved, pleased she hadn't been wrong, still bothered about Rebecca, but feeling as though she were floating on a cloud. 'I think you felt that way too?'

She nodded shyly. 'I couldn't believe, though, that you felt like that about someone like me.'

'Someone like you, Libby? Someone with a rare beauty that reminds me of an English rose? Rebecca's an exotic hothouse bloom, loved by some but not to everyone's taste, and especially not mine. You are truly re-markable—as delicate as a wild orchid. No man ought to be without someone like you.'

His compliments bemused her. She felt sure she wasn't worthy of any of them, but they were satisfying all the same, and she felt much more comfortable about staying. 'I'll fetch my clothes,' she said awkwardly.

'No need,' he told her. 'Your case is already here.' And when she gasped he said with a disarming smile, 'I anticipated you'd agree, and took the liberty of picking it up while I was out earlier. I trust you don't mind?'

Libby did mind, she minded very much, but she felt that under the circumstances it would be childish to protest.

He detected her anger instantly, and his voice was at its most cajoling. 'Libby, don't be cross; this is the best solution all round.'

'You could have asked me first,' she protested fiercely, her eyes deeply purple.

'It didn't occur to me until I was out, and I thought it would save wasting time later.' He pulled a little-boy face, the face of a boy who was trying to get back into his parent's good books. 'Do you forgive me?'

How could she not when he looked at her like that? 'I suppose so,' she agreed, 'but it doesn't mean to say I like what you did. It was a sneaky trick.' But already she was smiling. It pleased her to think that he was so sure of her, because she was just as sure of him.

He stood up and held out his hands. 'Come here, Libby.'

Without hesitation she walked into his arms. Already it felt the right thing to do. Confidence had grown in her, even though she still found it absolutely amazing that he should find her attractive when no other boy had looked at her twice. It was obviously true what they said about beauty being in the eye of the beholder. And, although outwardly she had not changed, inside she felt beautiful and feminine and sexy, and every one of her senses was responding to him.

She wanted him to hold her close, to kiss her, she craved real physical contact, but all he did was hold her very gently and look into her eyes. He seemed to be searching deep inside her, and his expression was as evocative as a kiss. The longer he looked at her, the more she responded. Tiny hidden tremors ran through her until her whole body sang with sensation. She would not have believed it possible to feel this way without being touched.

'You're beautiful, Libby,' he murmured and then, to her intense disappointment, he put her from him. 'I think a nightcap's in order. What will it be, a tot of whisky or rum, or——?'

'Just some orange juice, please,' said Libby, and in-stantly felt like an unsophisticated teenager. But she really wasn't 'into' drinking alcohol and, besides, she wanted to keep a clear head. He all too easily made her forget Rebecca.

He took a carton from a refrigerator, which was cleverly hidden behind a polished wooden door, and filled a glass. Her mouth was so dry that she drank it swiftly and gratefully. Then she went down into the galley and washed up.

Seeming to sense that she needed time to herself, Warwick stayed in the saloon, but, even so, Libby could still feel his presence. His male odour lingered on her skin, and she insanely wished that he weren't such a gentleman.

'I think I'll go to bed,' she said hesitantly when she had finished, needing to put some distance between them if she didn't want to torture herself further.

Warwick was stretched out on one of the dove-grey seats, his glass empty, his expression carefully guarded. 'Goodnight, Libby,' he murmured softly.

He still made her name sound different, and she wanted more than anything to go across the room and have him take her into his arms again, but she hated the thought that she could be making a fool of herself. Although he seemed to be genuinely attracted to her, she was too inexperienced in the ways of men to be sure. Besides, what she admired about him most was his restraint. She felt safe with him as things stood, and if she encouraged his kisses who knew what might happen?

She smiled weakly. 'Goodnight, Warwick.'

When she looked at her reflection in the bedroom mirror she was shocked to see the sparkle in her eyes and the flush on her cheeks. She looked like a different person. Who would have believed that one man, a stranger, in fact, could be capable of doing this to her? He could melt her at a touch or a glance. Simply thinking about him made the blood race through her veins. It was mind-boggling. But she was also very tired and, without bothering to unpack, she pulled a nightdress out of her case and got ready for bed.

The instant she slipped beneath the quilt she was asleep. She dreamed about Warwick—wonderful, erotic dreams where he was making endless love to her and telling her over and over again how beautiful she was. She awoke at the crack of dawn with his name on her lips, and for a few seconds felt deliriously happy, until the movement of the boat and the steady hum of its engine told her that they were no longer tied up in the harbour. They were on the move!

Instantly unease took the place of happiness, and she sprang out of bed. This man she had trusted—what was he doing? What was happening? Where were they going? What the devil was going on?

CHAPTER THREE

THE saloon was empty when Libby rushed up. There was no Warwick at the controls, no Warwick to watch or diagnose the meaningless pictures on the radar screen. And yet they were moving! Through the windows she could see nothing but open sea. They had obviously been going for some time.

The brief flicker of panic when she thought she was alone subsided when she realised Warwick must be up on the flybridge. She had asked him about it yesterday when he had shown her over the *Estoque*. She had felt like an ignorant fool when he'd told her that it was a duplicate set of controls.

Out of the saloon she hurried up the short, vertical ladder. The metal rungs were hard on her bare feet, the fresh wind billowing out her short cotton nightdress, but she was heedless of everything except her need to find out what was going on.

He sat at the wheel, his back to her, his dark hair ruffled, completely oblivious to the fact that she had come up behind him. When she spoke his name he turned his head, and she was shocked by the grimness of his face. 'So, you're awake!' he rasped harshly.

For just a second Libby froze, wondering what had happened to bring about this change, but the next instant she was at his side, arms akimbo, purple eyes flashing. 'Yes, I'm up, and I want to know what you think you're doing?'

'I have business to attend to in Lanzarote,' he told her calmly.

' "Business"?' she shrieked. 'At a time like this? How about Rebecca? Aren't you forgetting her?' This was a different Warwick Hunter from the sensual man she had met on the plane, the man who had held her in his arms last night and made her feel as though she was the most beautiful woman in the whole world. He was cool and distant, giving her the distinct impression that she was the one in the wrong, almost as though she were his enemy, which was crazy in the circumstances.

'How can I forget your dear sister and what she has done to me?' The sunglasses he wore prevented her seeing his eyes, but his caustic tone told her that there was no warmth in them. She guessed they were cold as ice, hard as flint, and directed straight at her.

' "Done to you"?' she queried, feeling a faint chill ride down her spine. 'What are you talking about?'

'I think it's time you knew what your precious Rebecca's been up to.'

Libby frowned. Something was obviously going on that she knew nothing about, something involving both Rebecca *and* Warwick. Perhaps he even knew where she was!

'Sit down,' he said tersely, indicating the padded seat next to him.

With only the slightest hesitation Libby did as he asked. She did wonder whether she ought to go back down and change, but she was too strung up, too impatient to hear what he had to say about her sister to worry too much about what she was wearing. Her vulnerability was the last thing on her mind. Though it was impossible not to feel faintly disturbed when she was sitting so close to him that their shoulders almost touched.

He slowed the engine and switched to auto-pilot so that he could give her his full attention. 'Whether this will come as a surprise to you, I'm unsure. You obviously know your sister far better than I do. In fact I suspect that you're here on the pretext that you're looking for her, yet all the time planning to pull the same kind of stunt.'

'I haven't a clue what you're talking about,' Libby said sharply, her frown deepening. 'All I want to know is why we're going to Lanzarote when my sister is missing. We should be looking for her, not messing about like this. Unless she's there? Is that what——?'

'Be quiet, Elizabeth!' he rasped.

The sharpness of his tone and his use of her proper name actually stunned her into silence. What had happened to turn him into this cold, hard-faced, accusing man? What had her sister done?

His lips were turned down at the corners as he spoke, and his eyes must be frozen into chips of grey ice. 'Rebecca, whom you profess to be so worried about, is enjoying herself somewhere with a considerable sum of money which rightfully belongs to me. She's been missing for over a week now.'

Libby gasped, her face suddenly draining of all colour. 'You're saying my sister has stolen money from you?' And when he nodded gravely and firmly she snapped, 'Becky wouldn't do a thing like that. She isn't a thief. How dare you accuse her? This is a ghastly mistake. There has to be some other explanation—some perfectly simple explanation.'

'If there is one, then I've yet to find it,' he thrust back savagely, his eyes cutting into her with their icy sharpness. 'And until such time as I come up with an answer, or get my money back, or get my hands on Rebecca——' each statement was accentuated with a closed fist punching the control board in front of him '—then *you* are staying with me!'

Libby was too anxious about her sister for the full import of what he'd said to sink in. 'I don't believe this about Becky!' she cried. 'You're lying, you're making it up.' Lord, how could he even think it? Rebecca might have her faults, but stooping so low as to steal from her employer wasn't one of them.

'Why should I make it up?' he asked coldly.

'My sister isn't a thief,' she riposted. 'If there is money missing, then I'm quite confident that she hasn't taken it.'

'*You* are confident?' he bit out scornfully. 'It would appear you don't know your sister as well as you think you do. If you're that certain, then how do you account for the fact that it disappeared at the same time as Rebecca?'

'It could be coincidence,' she returned, shivering despite the warmth of the day, folding her arms across her chest and rocking backwards and forwards on her seat.

'Too much of a damn coincidence,' he snorted. 'No, your sister took the money all right, and I sure as hell am going to make her suffer as soon as I catch up with her! Meanwhile you'll do very nicely.'

Libby was too dazed to think clearly. She kept shaking her head and looking at Warwick with wide, horrified eyes, at the same time rubbing her chilled arms with icy fingers. 'It has to be a mistake.'

'A mistake, yes, on your sister's part,' he rasped. 'I think she took me for some kind of fool.'

'And the police are looking for her?' she whispered, suddenly remembering all too clearly that time the policewoman had called at their house and told her that Rebecca was wanted in connection with a robbery. She had felt as if the whole world had suddenly crashed down over her head, and in the hours until it had proved to be a false alarm she had felt physically ill.

'Naturally,' he said grimly. 'But I'm not a patient man. I decided to do a little detective work myself.'

Libby felt as though her heart was going to force its way out of her chest. She had set out on this holiday so happily, and now, in the space of a few short hours, her whole world had turned upside-down. She still couldn't believe it; in fact she refused to believe it. Rebecca would never do such a thing; she was as sure of that as she had been of anything in her life.

'Unfortunately,' he went on resolutely, 'I've had no success so far in tracing Rebecca. I'm hoping that you can tell me where she is?'

'Me?' squeaked Libby. 'How can I tell you? I was expecting to find her on this boat!'

'You'd not arranged to meet her elsewhere?'

'Of course not.'

'She hadn't asked you to come and pick up those dresses that she left?'

'Most definitely not,' snapped Libby. 'Really, this is all getting beyond a joke.'

'I find it odd that you've come out here at the exact time that she has gone missing.'

'And I find it odd that she's gone missing at all!' Libby's eyes were a disturbed mauve, heavy with dread and deeply distrustful now of this man who was asking her all these questions. She suddenly wondered about their meeting. It all seemed too contrived, as though he had known all along who she was, as though he had engineered the whole thing.

'Our meeting wasn't accidental, was it?' she asked sharply, her eyes intent on his face, watching for every nuance, no matter how subtle.

He shook his head. 'No, it wasn't.'

She had thought he would deny it, and was shocked by the easy admission. 'You mean to say you planned to take me prisoner all along?' Her skin crawled at the thought that she had played right into his hands. How could she have been so naïve? She ought to have known that a man like Warwick Hunter wouldn't look twice at a girl like her. She sprang to her feet and glared down at him. 'You swine; how dare you? What you've done is tantamount to abduction. It's illegal. If I went to the police you'd be in deep, deep trouble.'

'And your sister's going to be in deep, deep trouble when they catch her,' he countered coldly.

Libby wondered how she had ever thought he had a sensual mouth. With lips tightly compressed, it was a vicious straight line. A muscle kept jerking in his jaw and his hands held the wheel in a grip tight enough to make his knuckles white.

'How did you do it? How did you find out that I'd be on that plane?' she asked hoarsely.

'Perhaps more luck than judgement,' he admitted. 'I had business in England, and decided to have a watch kept on your house in case Rebecca decided to run back home.'

Libby gasped. It was not pleasant knowing that her every movement had been monitored by a complete stranger.

'I didn't really think she would—not with all that money; it would be too risky. Then I was told that you were heading for Gatwick Airport. What else could I think but that you were going to meet her?'

'How did you know I was Rebecca's sister? I could have been a friend—anyone.' Libby was still shivering at the thought of being spied on.

'Rebecca once showed me your photograph. There are not many girls about with ash-blonde hair like yours. It really was just a matter of finding out which flight you were on. I must admit I was shocked that you were going to Tenerife. I thought Rebecca would have long since left the island.'

'And very fortunate for you that there was an available seat,' she thrust angrily. How easily he had duped her! She went cold even thinking about it. All the time he had known exactly who she was, all the time he had been planning to make her his prisoner. And he had gone about it in such a devious manner that she had agreed to sleep here of her own free will. He had not had to exert any force at all. The blood chilled in her veins at the very thought.

'I can assure you,' she snapped, 'that I haven't the slightest idea at all where Rebecca is. Did you tell the police yesterday that I was here?'

'I didn't actually go to see them,' he admitted coolly. 'They have their methods; I have mine. I'm actually quite enjoying this game. I'm looking forward to the pleasure of making you suffer.'

'You're out of your mind!' she spat. 'You can't keep me prisoner for ever.' He looked coldly sinister in his dark glasses, and she had never felt so frightened in her life, but her chin jutted and she glared at him fiercely. 'In any case, what were you doing with so much money on the boat? You ought to have had more sense.'

'They were the takings from one of my restaurants,' he informed her coolly.

Libby's brows rose. She had wondered what he did for a living. 'I still think it was pretty stupid leaving money lying around. It would be temptation for anyone.'

'It was in my safe,' he rasped.

Libby swallowed hard. So it definitely hadn't been taken on impulse; the whole affair must have been planned. 'You keep laying the blame on Becky,' she snapped, 'but I don't think it was her at all. Judging by those dresses in her wardrobe, she isn't short of money. Why should she feel the need to steal?'

'And how did she buy those clothes?' Warwick sneered. 'Have you noticed that they have designer labels? My guess is that I'm not the only person to have fallen prey to her light fingers.'

Libby's breath hissed out in anger and, swinging her arm in an arc, she slapped him across the face. 'You bastard! You know nothing. Becky isn't a thief; she would never do a thing like that. You're wrong, you're very wrong, and I hate you for even suggesting it. If she'd been planning to run away she would have taken everything with her.'

'Then you tell me where she is now, and where my money is? Normally my manager takes it to the night-safe at the bank, but he was away, ill, so I brought it home, planning to bank it myself the next morning. As it happened I was called away early and when I got back—bang!—both it and your sister had gone.'

Libby had to admit that it looked suspicious, but she was still confident that he was wrong. 'You're only surmising it was Becky,' she snapped.

'There is no other assumption,' he insisted icily. 'That money wasn't the first thing to go missing after she began working for me.'

'What do you mean?' choked Libby. 'What are you saying?' It got worse by the minute.

'A watch, a ring, a cigarette-lighter. Odd little things, things I thought I'd mislaid until the money went missing and I began to put two and two together.'

Libby began to feel ill. It couldn't be true, she wouldn't let it be true, but what other explanation was there? Without another word she scrambled to her feet and bolted back down to her cabin. Her whole body trembled with cold and fear and worry as she perched herself on the edge of the bed. She still refused to accept that her sister had stolen Warwick's money, and yet all the evidence was against her.

Would Warwick turn Rebecca over to the police if he found her? Would she be sent to prison? Or if the money was returned would he drop all charges and let them both go home? Could he do that now that it had been reported? None of the consequences bore thinking about.

How easily she had played right into his hands. He had trapped her with soft words and kisses, and she had fallen for it hook, line and sinker. Why, why, why hadn't she been suspicious? Didn't it make sense that, if no boy at home was interested in her, a good-looking man like Warwick Hunter, who could probably have his pick of any girl, wouldn't spare her even a passing glance? She really was a prize idiot. How he must have laughed behind her back!

Libby tried to think what her fate would be now. What he intended doing with her, *to* her! How long was he planning to keep her his prisoner? She closed her eyes and shivered. There was only one thing of which she was certain: Warwick Hunter wouldn't touch her again; he wouldn't need to put himself through the purgatory of pretending to like a woman who hadn't an ounce of sex appeal.

To give him his due, he had put on a good act, but that was all it had been, she knew that now, and he would undoubtedly feel relieved that the farce was over and he could treat her with the contempt he felt she deserved.

There was no doubt about it—she must escape, as soon as possible, and she must do all in her power to try to find her sister. It might be best to go back home in case Rebecca tried to contact her there. Already two days had gone by since she'd left. What if her sister had been telephoning? What if she really was in some kind of trouble, and needed her help—nothing to do with Warwick's money, but something else altogether?

Still feeling chilled through to her marrow, Libby tugged off her nightdress and took a hot shower before pulling on her jeans and T-shirt again. She did not even contemplate unpacking. At the very first opportunity she would escape. She must be ready at all times.

Again she looked at her sister's clothes in the wardrobe, and again she felt uneasy. Rebecca most certainly wouldn't willingly have left these behind. Such expensive clothes would mean a lot to her. She hadn't gone of her own free will, that was for sure. But, if she hadn't, where was she? What had happened to her?

Libby pulled open the top drawer of the dressing-table, expecting to see her sister's sexy underwear, and was taken aback when she discovered it was empty. Every drawer was empty! There was nothing at all except those few dresses in the wardrobe. No shoes, no handbag or passport, no money, no shorts, suntops or bikinis. Nothing!

It suddenly put a whole new complexion on the picture. Libby asked herself angrily why she hadn't thought to look in the drawers last night. Why had she assumed that because of the dresses everything else would still be there? It looked now as though Rebecca's departure had indeed been planned. Perhaps she hadn't had room for those dresses? Perhaps she had thought it would be easier to buy new ones?

Libby felt faint, and sat down. Everything was transpiring now to make her sister look guilty, and she did not want to believe it; in fact she refused to believe it. There was still some other explanation—there had to be; it was just a matter of finding it.

She sat a long time before venturing out into the galley, where she made herself a cup of tea she did not drink and toast she did not eat. She thought of Warwick up there on the flybridge, and found it difficult to believe that the only man she had ever found exciting was now her biggest enemy.

The way he had looked at her a few minutes ago, the way he had spoken, the way his whole body had rejected her, was like a nightmare in itself. They had been so close the day before, emotionally as well as physically, and she had been sure he felt the same. Now she knew that he was simply a very good actor.

Crawling out on to the deck, Libby prayed the sunshine would inject some heat into her icy limbs. At this moment she felt that she would never be warm again. She remained sitting with her back against the cabin, her hands around her knees, until they reached Lanzarote. She had no wish at all to speak to Warwick again.

He carefully nosed the boat into a harbour that was much smaller than the marina at Puerto Colon, but as soon as he came down to tie up Libby disappeared into her cabin. Within minutes her door banged open. 'Get your bag,' he said brusquely.

'I'll stay here,' she snapped back.

'And run away the moment my back's turned? I'm not that much of a fool, Elizabeth. I've arranged for a friend of mine to look after you while I conduct my business.'

As if I were a child! she thought angrily. 'If you're that worried I'll escape, why don't you take me with you?' she yelled, her purple eyes flashing. 'Or lock me in. Wouldn't that be a better proposition?' It seemed more in keeping with the type of man he was turning out to be.

He did not answer. With her wrist firmly clamped in one of his big hands, he marched her off the boat, and she had to trot to keep up with his long strides.

'This is ridiculous,' she cried. 'Let go of me; you're hurting!'

'We're almost there,' he barked, and although his fingers relaxed he still maintained his hold on her.

Libby had never felt so humiliated in her life, and yet, despite everything, she still managed to feel the pull of his magnetism. It was weird the way he had this stranglehold over her. It was almost as though he had hypnotised her, as though, whatever happened, however he treated her, she would always feel something for him.

They stopped at a small, white, box-like house, with cacti growing in a garden that was walled by lava stones and mulched with black volcanic cinders. The green door opened as they approached, and a black-haired woman, probably in her early forties, smiled warmly at Warwick. She had startlingly white teeth and laughing eyes, and was very beautiful. He let Libby go, and took the woman into his arms. 'It's good to see you again, Maria.'

Libby surprised herself by feeling a stab of jealousy. In the circumstances it shouldn't have bothered her however many women he kissed, but it did, and she turned away. The next instant his hand was on her arm again and she was being introduced. 'Elizabeth, this is Maria Martén; Maria, Elizabeth Eaton, the girl I told you about.'

They shook hands, the woman's smile genuinely warm and welcoming. 'Off you go, Warwick,' she said with a laugh. 'Elizabeth will be perfectly all right with me.'

Libby wondered exactly what he had said to this attractive woman. Had he told her that she was not to be let out of her sight for one second in case she disappeared? Did the woman know the true situation?

Expecting to be shut inside the house until Warwick returned, Libby was pleasantly surprised when Maria suggested they walk along the pleasant waterfront. 'This is Playa Blanca,' she said, 'although I expect Warwick's told you all about it?'

'Actually, no,' confessed Libby.

Maria looked surprised. 'Well, we're on the southern coast of Lanzarote, and this was a small, quiet fishing village until tourism began to creep here as well. It's good for the economy, but not so good for the locals. The ferry for Fuerteventura leaves from here; look, you can see the island. The beaches there are incredible. And this is Warwick's restaurant.' Maria indicated a white building with blue paintwork and blue and white striped umbrellas over the tables. There were plenty of people sitting drinking, talking, laughing, but Warwick himself was nowhere in sight.

Libby could not help thinking how well situated the restaurants were here. A low wall was all that divided them from the beach, and she could imagine sitting here at night when the area was dimly lit, listening to the sound of the ocean, watching the candles flickering on the tables. And in her mind's eye it was Warwick she saw herself with. She cast the thought aside angrily, and was relieved when Maria suggested they go for a drive.

'I don't want to put you out,' said Libby. 'I really don't know why Warwick imposed me on you. I could easily have stayed on the boat.'

'Warwick did not want you to get bored,' smiled the woman easily. 'I don't mind, really I don't. It's a change for me to be able to do something for him. He was such a comfort when my husband died four years ago—a great source of strength and support. I'm over it now. My children are growing up, and I feel I can get on with my life.'

Maria's English was excellent, and as Libby climbed into her car she felt that she would have liked to be friends with this woman—in different circumstances!

'There has never been any romance between me and Warwick, you understand,' said Maria as she headed away from her house. 'He is like a brother, and that is how I love him. But I sense that there is something between you two. Am I right?' Libby glanced at her with startled eyes. 'You don't have to tell me,' laughed Maria. 'I shouldn't pry, I know, but I'm interested. It's the first time Warwick's ever done anything like this. How did you two meet?'

'Hasn't he told you?' asked Libby.

Maria shook her head. 'He told me nothing except that he had a friend staying with him and he did not want to leave her by herself. What's happened to the girl who used to do his cooking and cleaning?'

'That was my sister,' said Libby, seeing no reason why she shouldn't disclose the truth, or at least part of it. She would have liked to tell Maria everything, and enlist her help to escape. But it was easy to see the woman thought a lot of Warwick, and would remain loyal to him. It was probably why he had chosen her.

'I actually came out on a surprise visit,' she confessed, 'but she—er—put in her notice and left before I got here and, well, Warwick said I could stay with him for a few days.'

'I see,' said Maria. 'What a shame that you came all this way for nothing. There's probably a letter for you at home giving you her new address. But never mind; think what a lovely holiday you're having. Warwick's a wonderful person, so kind and generous. It's just like him to suggest you stay on his boat. You really couldn't have met a nicer person.'

So long as you're on the right side of him, thought Libby bitterly. It was obvious Maria had never seen him in a black mood. 'Why hasn't he ever married?' she asked—if he was the epitome of such perfection! She found it very strange that at the age of thirty-four he was still a single man.

'He doesn't talk much about himself,' answered Maria, 'but I believe there was once a girl whom he loved very much. I understand they were about to be married when she suddenly died—and he's not been interested in any girl since—not seriously. There have been girls, yes, but none of them has struck the right chord. I wonder if you could be the one?'

Her smile was impish, but Libby shook her head. 'There's nothing like that between us, I assure you.'

'It's early days yet,' grinned Maria.

Libby did not enlighten her.

The black volcanic landscape was beautiful rather than desolate, as she had imagined. She saw grapes growing abundantly in pockets of ash protected from the harsh winds by semi-circular walls of lava stone. She saw tourists riding on camels, donkeys laden with crops, old women dressed all in black with white straw hats on their heads.

There were lots of things to see, but not enough time, and she was given a whistle-stop tour which whetted her appetite but did not curb it. Perhaps one day, when all this was over, she would be able to come here again and explore Lanzarote properly.

Instead of going back to her house Maria drove to the harbour, and Warwick was already there. He smiled warmly at Maria, and invited her on board for a drink. Libby envied them their easy camaraderie, and was surprised the dark-haired woman wasn't in love with him. Who could fail to resist his special brand of sexuality? Hadn't she fallen instantly in love with him herself? And yet Maria seemed sublimely unaware of it, joking and laughing and treating him just like the big brother she had declared.

As she took her leave Maria made Libby promise to pay her a visit if she was ever in Lanzarote again, and as soon as her car was out of sight the ropes were untied and the *Estoque* headed back towards Tenerife.

Warwick's mood abruptly changed. The cheerfulness he had shown Maria turned to black, brooding anger— it was there in the darkening of his face and the narrowed hardness of his eyes. It was impossible to believe that there had ever been any awareness or warmth between them, and the more she thought about the way he had tricked her, the more furious Libby grew.

There had to be a way to escape this man; he could not keep her prisoner here for ever. It was simply a matter of biding her time, waiting for the right opportunity. Meanwhile, it was still hot enough to sunbathe. Why waste this glorious sunshine?

She had packed a bikini, one of Rebecca's cast-offs, a black and pink creation that was only just decent and, donning it now, she lay down on a towel on the deck. But she couldn't relax; she couldn't get out of her mind the fact that Warwick had planned all along to make her his prisoner. She had thought him such a wonderful man. How stupid she had been, how incredibly stupid! Her hands clenched into fists at her side. How she wished she were a man. She would go up there and knock him for six!

It had not occurred to Libby that he would be able to see her from up on the flybridge. It was not until she felt the sensation of eyes upon her that she realised she was in his full view. If she had lain a yard or so further back she would have been hidden. Another mistake! But there was no point in moving, giving him the pleasure of knowing that however much she hated him he still had the power to disturb her. That really would provide ammunition for his gun.

The longer she lay there the more uncomfortable she became, but still she did not move; instead she turned on to her stomach so that she wasn't tempted to glance up at him. But the knowledge that he was watching her did not go away, and her veins raced with a warmth that had nothing at all to do with the sun, and which angered her beyond measure. He was an out-and-out swine, so why was she feeling this way?

And the warmth developed into an ache, an actual physical need for him, which appalled her. She scrambled to her feet. It was no good; she could not stay here a second longer. As she did so she looked up and his eyes were upon her still, a grim smile of satisfaction on his lips, as though he knew what he was doing to her. Libby was furious, and she glared and then almost tripped over her towel.

She stamped her way back to her cabin, showered, and changed into one of her home-made cotton dresses, and stayed there until they reached Tenerife. It infuriated her that she could still feel like this when he was treating her so atrociously. What was the matter with her? Had she gone crazy? Had she let this man go to her head? OK, so he excited her physically, but surely she could handle that? All she had to remember was that he was her enemy, that he was keeping her prisoner here against her will. Wasn't that sufficient to banish these unwanted feelings?

Seconds after he had tied up he banged on her door. 'Elizabeth, come out here.' His tone was harsh and commanding, and it was easy then to hate him.

'What for? What do you want?' she yelled.

'I want something to eat.'

'And you think I'm going to cook it? I may be your prisoner, Warwick, but I'm not your slave. Cook it yourself!'

The door bounced open, and he stood there, tall and forbidding, a thatch of dark hair falling over his forehead, his eyes inky dark and directed straight at her. 'You'll do whatever I ask.'

It was difficult facing up to him. Libby had never met a man as intimidating as Warwick before. Nevertheless she lifted her chin and eyed him bravely. 'And if I don't?'

'I wouldn't advise you to defy me. Things will only get worse if you don't do as I say. Until such time as Rebecca is found you'll cook and clean and do everything else that your sister did.' His eyes were hard and grey on hers. 'It will be small recompense for what she has taken, but for the moment it will have to do. Perhaps I ought to warn you that I make a formidable enemy.'

'That much I'd already gathered,' she told him smartly, 'and, as I happen to be hungry myself, perhaps I will cook dinner. Excuse me.' She was trying to appear nonchalant, as though his harsh words did not bother her, even though inside she was seething, but as she attempted to push past him his arm shot across the doorway and barred her exit.

Her eyes went up to his, a word of protest on her lips, her heart thudding an instant response. She was so close she could feel the heat of his body and see every pore on his face, but, as his arms whipped around her and pulled her hard against him, she fought with every ounce of her strength. 'Stop it! What the hell do you think you're doing?'

'What am I doing?' Warwick's smile was without humour. 'Don't you know? Do I have to spell it out for you? What a little hell-cat you've suddenly become. Do keep still.'

'Let me go and I will,' she snapped, increasing her struggles.

'Not until I'm good and ready.' His voice was like steel. 'You're mine now, Libby; haven't you realised that yet? As security for the money Rebecca stole, you're mine in every sense of the word.'

When his mouth came down on hers Libby knew exactly what he meant.

CHAPTER FOUR

IT WAS impossible for Libby to stop the trigger of excitement that shot through her when Warwick's lips touched hers, but that did not mean she was going to accept his kiss—or anything else he might feel like doing! Oh, no, he was not going to get away with anything like that.

Anger and indignation gave her the strength to wrench free, and she backed out into the galley, wishing there were somewhere else to run. 'Don't you dare touch me, Warwick Hunter,' she snapped. 'I'm not yours, not now, not ever. Whatever you think Rebecca might have done, it doesn't give you the right to manhandle me.'

'Aren't you cutting off your nose to spite your face?' His eyes were hard, his jaw taut.

'I'm doing what any self-respecting girl would do in the circumstances.' Every muscle in Libby's body was tightened to exploding-point, and she sought the cool metal of the fridge door behind her. When she had set out on her journey to visit Rebecca she had never anticipated that anything like this would happen. How wrong she had been in her assumption that he wouldn't want to touch her again.

Ironically, she had on occasions wished for excitement. A hairdresser's life was often mundane, and more especially since Rebecca had left home had she felt that she was in a rut. But never in her wildest dreams had she imagined anything so devastating as this.

In two strides Warwick was in front of her, cold blue-grey eyes staring into hers, effectively pinning her to the spot. Libby felt the blood scream through her veins, every hair on her body rising in protest. Her eyes looked wildly about her for some weapon should he dare try to touch her again.

'You can't deny, Libby, that there's a certain chemical something between us.' It was 'Libby' again now, said with that deliberate emphasis that had once set her nerve-ends tingling.

'Rubbish!' Her eyes were frozen orbs of polished amethyst, and her blood had turned to ice. 'It's all been an act as far as you're concerned. I'm the one who's been taken in, I'm the fool. But no longer, I assure you. Every single emotion I felt has gone, and I'm left with nothing but hatred, pure hatred.'

He hadn't moved a muscle; there was not even a flicker in his eyes to suggest that her words had got through to him.

She drew in a deep breath and continued her tirade. 'You're despicable the way you've gone about things, the way you duped me into thinking that we were at the beginning of some wonderful, rare relationship. What a naïve idiot I was. I appear to be in a no-win situation at the moment, but you dare lay a finger on me and you'll realise I'm more than a hell-cat—you'll wish you'd never even met me!'

Muscles twitched in his jaw. 'Are you throwing down the gauntlet?'

'Challenging you is the last thing I would do,' she retorted. 'All I'm saying is keep your hands off. For the moment I'll cook our meals and keep the boat clean, but that's as far as I'm prepared to go. If you want a woman in your bed you'd better find someone else.'

'What if I say I don't want anyone else, that I want you?'

'Then you'll be in for a big disappointment.' Her breathing was rapid now, her breasts rising and falling, thrusting against the thin fabric of her dress—and he did not fail to notice. The way he looked at her, a long, slow, calculated appraisal, was as intimate as if he were actually touching her, and to her shame she felt her breasts harden in response. She swung away, disgusted with herself. 'I have no intention of being treated as a plaything.'

'You do me an injustice, Libby. That wasn't my intention at all.' To her intense relief he moved to one side, a foot on the steps leading up to the saloon. 'I've never forced myself on any woman, and I don't intend to start now. Whatever happens between us, you'll want it as much as me, make no bones about that.'

Libby gasped at his audacity, but before she could make any sort of response he had bounded up the steps and she heard him cross the saloon to his own cabin at the opposite end of the boat. She took a deep, steadying breath. It would take a bulldozer to push her into his arms!

The air was filled with tension as they sat down for their meal. Warwick was coldly withdrawn, and Libby, who had been expecting him to make further advances, had erected an icy façade. It was a waste of time. She might not have been there for all the notice he took of her, and the instant he finished eating he retreated back to his cabin.

Libby washed up and then sat outside. It was dark now, but still warm, and there were lots of holiday-makers milling around. All as free as the air!

She thought about Rebecca. It just wasn't possible that her sister would have stolen such a large sum of money. There had to be some other explanation. Wild though Rebecca sometimes was, she had never committed any criminal offence, and there was no reason why she should start now. She did not believe that those dresses in her wardrobe had been bought with ill-gotten gains.

What if Rebecca had gone home? What if she was there now, worrying because she, Libby, was missing? No sooner was the thought born than Libby reacted. Going back to her cabin, she picked up her purse, so anxious about Rebecca that she did not even give a thought to the fact that she was Warwick's prisoner. But no sooner had she stepped off the boat than he appeared in the cockpit, proving beyond any shadow of doubt that he was monitoring her movements. His face was dark with anger. 'Where the hell do you think you're going?'

Libby's chin jutted as she met the icy glitter in his eyes. 'To phone home. I thought I'd see if Rebecca's there.'

His suspicion did not fade. 'An excellent idea, but what's wrong with my radio telephone?'

'Nothing,' she said at once. 'I didn't know it could be used for long-distance calls. I thought it was simply to contact shore whenever you were going into port.'

'It can be used,' he confirmed grimly, getting her the necessary line and then standing at her side, as impatient as she to find out if Rebecca was there.

But the phone rang out emptily the other end, and disappointedly Libby replaced the receiver. 'So that's that,' she said on a heavy sigh. 'I wish I knew where she was; I'm desperately worried about her.'

'Why, when she's probably having the time of her life spending *my* money?' he gibed drily. 'She'll probably wait until she's spent it all before going home.' His hands were thrust into his trouser pockets, the fine linen material pulled taut, his powerfully muscled thighs attracting her attention.

Libby moved away from him, disturbed to feel reluctant desire flare to life inside her. It was unreal that he could do this to her when she hated him so much. Letting him get through to her on the plane had been her downfall. It was impossible now to banish these feelings.

'I refuse to accept that Rebecca took it,' she said crisply. 'No matter what you say, no matter how incriminating the circumstances are, I think you're wrong.' She wished he would stop looking at her with those intense smoky blue eyes that kicked everything inside her into life whether she wanted it or not.

'No one else knew the money was there,' he reminded her sardonically. 'It had to be Rebecca. As I've already pointed out, it would be too much of a coincidence for both her and the money to disappear at the same time.'

'And nothing I say will change your mind?'

'The only thing that will change my mind is if Rebecca returns and proves to me that she's innocent.'

'She could have got into bad company,' Libby stated firmly. 'It could be one of her friends who's taken it.'

Warwick shook his head impatiently. 'She never brought anyone back to the boat.'

'Maybe they came when you weren't here?'

'You're clutching at straws, Elizabeth. It was a one-off occasion that I had so much money in my safe. There was no time for anything premeditated.'

If Rebecca hadn't been her sister, Libby would have been inclined to agree with him, but in the circumstances she refused to believe it. It was so out of character. There had to be some other explanation. But what?

It was not until later when Libby put her purse back into her handbag that she discovered her passport was missing—both her passport and her return flight ticket.

It was not difficult to guess who had taken them. She marched back out into the saloon, her eyes bright with anger, her hand held out towards Warwick. 'I want my passport and ticket. You had no right taking them from my bag.'

'Without your passport I know you can't get far,' he told her cruelly. 'You'll get them back when I'm ready to let you go.'

There wasn't an ounce of compassion on his face, and not for the first time Libby wondered how he could be two such totally different people. He was a proper Jekyll and Hyde, though she doubted she would ever see again the caring person she had thought him on the plane. Was that the true side of him, or was this? She was beginning to realise how very little she knew about him. 'You cannot do this,' she cried angrily.

'Believe me, I've done it,' he told her. 'Your documents are locked away carefully in my safe, and you can bet your bottom dollar that you'll never be privy to its location. I've been stupid once, never again.'

Meaning Rebecca had known where it was, and had known either the combination or where the key was kept. But that still did not mean that her sister was the one who had broken into it. How could he accuse her of such a thing?

'I hate your guts,' she spat, because she could think of nothing else to say, and flounced back into her cabin.

All night long Libby racked her brains for a solution to the problem. Perhaps Zelda had something to do with Rebecca's disappearance? Perhaps she was in trouble, and Rebecca had gone to help her? There were a thousand and one questions and answers, but which was the correct one, and how would either of them know the truth until they saw Rebecca again?

She awoke heavy-eyed and dispirited, and to her amazement discovered she had the boat to herself. She assumed that now Warwick had her passport he was secure in the knowledge that she would not run away.

In any case, she had remembered in bed last night hinting to Rebecca a long time ago that she would try to save up for a holiday in Tenerife. Therefore, if Rebecca did try to contact her at home, and repeatedly got no answer, she might put two and two together and guess she was here.

On the other hand, if Rebecca had stolen the money, this boat was the last place she would show her face, but it was an unworthy thought. Rebecca was innocent, she was sure of it. Her sister would turn up without fail in a day or two, and wonder what all the fuss was about.

Now that she had no choice, Libby unpacked her case and hung away her clothes. Her home-made dresses looked pathetic beside the exotic creations Rebecca had left behind, and she held one or two in front of her, trying to imagine what she would look like in something so expensive.

Money had been tight ever since their parents died, and she'd had to save very hard to come out here. Not that she regretted it, and she was even more glad now that she had come because otherwise she would never have found out that Rebecca was missing. If only there was something she could do, some way she could find out where her sister had gone.

She dressed in a cotton skirt and T-shirt, and made herself some toast and coffee, which she took up on to the top deck, enjoying the lazy warmth of the early morning sun. In other circumstances, if she hadn't been so desperately worried about Rebecca, it would have been idyllic.

When she heard a female voice calling out Warwick's name her heart missed a beat as, for a second, she thought it might be her sister, and she started to her feet.

'Warwick, where are you?'

Disappointment struck. The low, husky voice was nothing like Rebecca's.

'Darling, are you up there?'

Libby looked over the rail, and almost laughed at the shock on the beautiful woman's face. In an instant the stranger had climbed the half-dozen or so rungs of the ladder and was standing on the platform beside Libby.

'Who are you and what are you doing here?' she demanded haughtily, frowning when she saw that Libby was alone.

'Libby Eaton, and I'm Warwick's house guest—or should I say boat guest?' It was rare that Libby disliked someone at first sight, but this disdainful woman with her jet-black hair and emerald-green eyes set her teeth on edge. She was actually very beautiful, with a perfect face and figure, fingernails long and polished, but her eyes were cold and there was an arrogant tilt to her head that Libby found offensive.

'You're—staying here?' The words were difficult for the other woman to get out. 'With Warwick?'

Libby nodded. 'That's right.'

'Since when, and for how long?' she demanded imperiously.

Libby felt her hackles rise. 'I don't see that it's any business of yours.'

Green eyes flashed. 'I intend making it mine. Warwick Hunter is a very close friend of many years' standing, and he's never mentioned you before.' Her black hair was drawn tightly back into a chignon, revealing her long, swan-like neck. She was probably about Warwick's age, very tall and slender with a willowy grace that made

Libby feel gauche. The white dress she wore was the epitome of elegance even at this time in the morning. Her red shoes matched her nails and lipstick, and a red shoulder-bag was slung carelessly over one shoulder.

'That's because I'm a very *new* friend,' answered Libby.

'And he's invited you to stay here on such a short acquaintance?' Her tone was incredulous.

Libby guessed that this elegant woman had been hankering after just such an invitation herself. Obviously it had not been forthcoming, and it amused her now not to tell her the real reason she was here. 'The attraction was instant and mutual,' she told her calmly. 'If you tell me your name I'll let Warwick know that you called.'

The woman's eyes narrowed to two cat-like slits. 'I'll wait, thank you. Where is he?'

'Out on business.' It was a calculated guess, but it could not be far from the truth.

The woman inclined her head. 'I'll be down in the saloon.' She turned to leave, and they both saw Warwick at the same time, standing on the ladder, head and shoulders only above deck.

Libby wondered how long he had been there, listening to their conversation, and hot colour suffused her cheeks. It was obvious that he hadn't been very far away and that her assumption that he was watching the boat had been right.

'Warwick!' said the woman in delight.

'Paula,' he acknowledged, hauling himself up the last couple of treads.

The woman draped herself around him with feline grace, paying no heed at all to Libby, who shocked herself by feeling raw jealousy rise in her throat. Jealousy, when she hated him? It did not make sense.

Maria had said there had been many girls in his life, but none of them serious. Paula looked very serious indeed. She was obviously in love with Warwick, and he was making no effort at all to push her away; in fact he appeared to be enjoying the feel of her in his arms, and when Paula lifted her face for his kiss it seemed to go on for ever.

Libby turned away, concentrating her attention on a red dinghy being lowered from one of the other boats, not looking at them again until Warwick spoke her name.

'Libby, did you two girls introduce yourselves?'

With reluctance she swung back, seeing the malevolent gleam in Paula's eyes as she stood with Warwick's arm still about her shoulders.

'I did,' she managed to say stiffly, 'but I have no idea who your friend is.'

His eyes narrowed slightly at the hardness of her tone, but when he looked down at Paula there was a softening of his expression as he pulled her closer to him. 'This is Paula Cameron. She's an extremely talented and clever woman. We flew out to the Canary Islands together, and our success rates have run in tandem with each other. She is now the proud owner of a string of very successful high-class dress shops across the islands.'

Which accounted for the way she was dressed now, thought Libby. Not for Paula anything casual, only something expensive and elegant, something which made her look like a million dollars—and didn't she know it!

'Libby didn't tell me how you two met?'

Paula's tone was softly enquiring, with just the right amount of interest, but Libby knew it was no casual question. This woman saw her as a rival in the stakes for Warwick Hunter.

Warwick smiled down at Paula. 'Libby and I also met on the plane coming out from England. Isn't that a co-incidence? She's Rebecca's sister; did she tell you that?'

Libby felt warning bells ring in her head. How much did Paula know about Rebecca? That she was missing? That there was money missing as well?

'Rebecca? Oh, yes.' Paula's eyes narrowed at the memory of the young girl who could well equal her in the glamour stakes. 'Where is she, by the way?'

So she didn't know! Libby felt relief, but her eyes froze as she met the dark humour in Warwick's.

'Rebecca's decided a change is as good as a rest,' he remarked. 'She's left me for shores unknown. Libby has taken her place.'

The woman frowned; this was something she clearly had not expected. 'You mean Libby is your—er—she is employed by you?'

'That's right,' announced Warwick, his eyes wickedly amused as he looked at Libby.

She felt like spitting in his eye. Employed by him indeed!

'In that case,' said Paula, her green eyes alight with malicious pleasure, 'I think she ought to make us both a cup of coffee. I'm simply dying for a drink, aren't you, darling? Let's sit here and enjoy the sunshine before it gets too hot.'

Libby did not wait for Warwick to speak. She did not want to hear him give his orders. She did not like to think that he was using her as his personal slave. He certainly wouldn't find her very submissive, that was a fact.

She filled the coffee-jug and plugged it in, all the time damning Warwick for the way he was treating her. The more she thought about her situation, the more her anger grew and, when Paula descended into the saloon on the pretext that she wanted to use Warwick's bathroom, Libby's eyes were a violent, glaring purple.

'I thought I ought to put you straight.' The woman's husky tones had lost the soft seductiveness she used when speaking to Warwick, and her eyes were a cool ice-green that washed over Libby contemptuously. 'It would appear that you have the wrong idea about you and Warwick. Your suggestion of "mutual attraction" is laughable. You might have a hang-up about him—what woman hasn't?—but he certainly feels nothing for you.'

'And he's told you that, has he?' countered Libby sharply.

'Warwick has asked me to marry him,' announced Paula in triumph. 'Of course it was always on the cards, though we've both been too busy to do anything about it. Until now. It's funny how we both met him on a plane, isn't it? Although I'm afraid you're about twelve years too late, my dear. Please hurry along with the coffee.'

Libby stood frozen, believing and yet not wanting to believe, and not until Paula disappeared did she recover sufficiently to gulp air into her tortured lungs. She discovered to her disgust that she was trembling, which was ridiculous. Why should it bother her that Warwick was going to marry Paula? She hated the man, didn't she? He was welcome to her.

Even if there hadn't been this trouble with Rebecca, Libby would never have been his type. Paula was sophisticated and intelligent and extremely good-looking. All of the qualities Libby wished she possessed but didn't. Never had she had it more vividly rammed home.

In any case, whatever feelings she had felt for him in the beginning were gone, weren't they? She hated him now. She felt absolutely nothing for him—except perhaps an unwanted animal attraction that she could easily control. Admittedly she'd been flattered because he was the first man to pay her so much attention. She had acted like a schoolgirl with a crush on her teacher instead of a mature twenty-three-year-old who ought to know better. But she was wiser now. He was detestable, he was the most hateful man she had ever met, and there was no way she was ever going to let him touch her again. His engagement to Paula was a blessing in disguise. She could throw it at him if he ever dared try anything on.

She was trembling so much that she knew she was not capable of carrying a tray, or even the cups one at a time up the ladder. Warwick would have to come down for them.

At the bottom she stood and called to him that their drinks were ready, and he took the two cups from her without so much as a smile. Tight-lipped, Libby went back inside.

There were several things she could do. She could get out the polish and duster, or the vacuum cleaner, or the cleaning materials for the bathrooms, but that would only confirm her position in Paula's eyes, and she had no intention of doing that.

She paced the room, she studied the dials and instruments, she looked at Warwick's log-book, she topped up the ice-maker, and she fumed—above all she fumed. It was an intolerable situation, and if Paula was going to be a regular visitor it would be even worse. The last thing she wanted was this arrogant woman being condescending towards her.

An hour later, to her intense relief, Paula announced that she was leaving. 'It's been very—er—interesting meeting you, Libby,' she said. 'Warwick does seem to have this penchant for picking up waifs and strays. I hope you're a better cook than your sister. The poor dear does need his nourishment.'

Warwick seemed not to notice the poison behind her words. 'You must dine here and see for yourself. How about tomorrow night?'

Libby's teeth smashed together so hard it was a wonder they didn't break. If he thought she was going to cook for them and watch Paula pouring herself all over him, he had another think coming!

'Darling, I'd love to,' whispered Paula, nibbling at his ear, one eye on Libby, watching closely her reaction, 'but I'm off this afternoon to Madrid to that fashion show I told you about. Did you forget?'

'For a moment.' His tone was as husky and soft as hers. 'We'll save the pleasure for another time.'

Libby watched as he walked Paula to her silver-grey Porsche Carrera—an expensive, classy car which suited its owner perfectly. A length of carefully tanned thigh was exposed as she slid in, and Warwick lowered his head to give her a goodbye kiss.

Libby swung away, tormented by the sight of the two dark heads together, and when Warwick returned she was busy with a duster and polish. Although she did not look at him, it amazed her how keenly she felt his presence. It was like being in a cold room and someone switching on the electric fire. Was it always going to be like this? Was she never going to get over that initial burst of love she had felt for him? Was it going to torment her for however long she was compelled to stay here?

'I have a table booked tonight at a new restaurant that has just opened,' he informed her. 'I trust you have something nice to wear?'

For a second Libby stilled, then she looked up into the hazy blue of his eyes, which were still soft with memories of Paula. 'Even if I had I wouldn't go with you,' she told him coldly. 'You can go on your own.'

'I think not.' There was no trace of the softness in his voice that he had used when speaking to Paula. 'There is no argument, Elizabeth; we are going whether you like it or not.'

Her head jerked and she eyed him defiantly. 'I'd like to clean your cabin if you're not using it.' What was the point in arguing when he would undoubtedly get his own way?

'Feel free,' he grated, his eyes hard now, his jaw like granite. 'I have paperwork to do, which will keep me busy for most of the day, but you're coming out with me tonight, make no mistake about that.' He disappeared through a door obliquely adjacent to his stateroom, which Libby had previously assumed was a bathroom. It was obvious now that it was his office.

Libby stood and fumed for a few minutes. It was an amazing situation. She hated him with every fibre of her being and yet she still felt an intense awareness. Even the air became difficult to breathe when he was around. What the hell was wrong with her? Was she so weak that she could not control her feelings?

'Damn you, Warwick Hunter!' she said beneath her breath as she entered his cabin. 'You have no right doing this to me.'

His bed dominated the state-room. It had a grey velvet padded headboard and a row of inset lights above. There were cabinets either side, a dressing-table and a wardrobe—and it was so tidy it was unbelievable. Not a thing was out of place. She stood for just a second taking it all in. It was so easy to imagine him here, sleeping in that bed, the harsh lines of his face relaxed.

She shook her head at the line her thoughts were taking, and ran the cleaner furiously over the floor, polishing the teak furniture with unnecessary vigour, trying all the time to keep her eyes off the bed.

She could not help wondering whether Paula had ever slept there, whether those two dark heads had shared the same pillow. It brought a swift, unwanted stab of pain to her throat, and she chastised herself for letting her imagination run riot.

One door in the corner revealed a toilet and wash-basin, and another door in the opposite corner a shower. She quickly wiped over the ceramic surfaces, sniffing appreciatively the lingering odour of the aftershave Warwick always used—a spicy, tangy smell that she knew would for ever remind her of him.

After she had finished Libby went up on to the fly-bridge, as far away from him as she could possibly get, and sunbathed on one of the covered padded mattresses that were there for that purpose. She was still deter-mined not to go tonight. What pleasure would either of them derive from it? If he wanted he could lock her on the boat; even that would be preferable to spending time with him.

As midday approached and it became unbearably hot, she went down and prepared a salad and sliced cold chicken, tapping on the office door when she had fin-ished. 'Lunch is ready.' Her voice was cool and unfriendly.

Warwick also was silently distant throughout the meal, and afterwards Libby asked him if she could take a walk around the harbour. 'I can't stay cooped up here without any form of exercise.'

He nodded his agreement. 'But I'll be watching you,' he grated, and the coldness in his eyes made her shiver.

Libby felt gloriously free as she walked away from the *Estoque*. She climbed a circular stone staircase, and looked down on the harbour from a path up above. The ground rose steeply, and a richly tiled pathway ran along the mile-long coast to Playa de las Américas itself. According to Warwick, it was lined with bars and restaurants and shopping-squares, and was a popular walk with holiday-makers, especially during the evenings, when live entertainment was provided to attract customers.

She looked in boutiques and a marvellous book shop, and when she got back Warwick was still apparently working, though she had no doubt that he had been carefully watching her movements. She took a shower and lay down, knowing nothing more until he banged on the door.

When she did not immediately answer he rudely pushed it open, stopping only when he saw her lying naked on the bed.

Libby was instantly wide awake, sitting up and attempting to cover herself with the sheet, feeling a sudden warmth spread through her limbs as his eyes seemed to rasp over the surface of her skin, and wishing she'd had the good sense to lock the door. She had thought only to lie for a few minutes, never dreaming that she would go to sleep. Lord, he was awakening a thousand tiny impulses all over her body! She was responding to him as surely as if he were touching her. Was she going out of her mind? What a crazy, stupid thing to happen.

'Am I to be allowed no privacy on this boat?' she demanded coldly, her eyes wide and protesting and yet hiding none of the emotions that were surging through her like a waterskier out of control. There was an actual luminous quality about her eyes which she was unaware of, but which did not go unnoticed by Warwick.

'It's time for you to get ready, Libby.' He once again said her name with that different inflexion from everyone else, and to her disgust his deep-timbred voice still had the power to melt her bones. It was like a gentle vibration right through every nerve. 'Unless you'd prefer to stay here?' His voice went down another octave and his eyes darkened to a deep navy blue.

And make love to her? Was that what he was suggesting? Her eyes flashed. What a swine the man was, when he had just asked another girl to marry him! Being engaged apparently made no difference. He still intended to make her pay for what he was sure Rebecca had done.

He leaned forward over the bed, one hand on each side of her body, electrifying her. 'It's either the restaurant, or you and me here.'

She closed her eyes for a second, taking deep, uneven breaths. 'Very well, I'll come.' How husky her voice sounded! Husky and shaky, telling him all too shamefully that she was having difficulty controlling her emotions. Heavens, what sort of a pathetic woman was she? He must have known what her answer would be. He had made the threat deliberately to scare her into accepting. 'If you'll let me up, I'll get ready.'

But Warwick was in no hurry to move. His eyes were hypnotic on hers, and she was breathing in the musky man-smell of him, dragging it into her lungs, feeling a tortured ache deep in her groin. *And he knew exactly what he was doing to her!*

CHAPTER FIVE

MUCH to Libby's disgust, a whole new world opened up for her, a world where senses mattered more than anything else. The longer Warwick looked at her, the more sensitised she became. Strangely, she could do nothing about it. She forgot he was her gaoler, her enemy, she forgot she hated him passionately. Her body became boneless, and she slipped back down the bed, her head resting on the pillow, her flushed face framed by the platinum whiteness of her hair. Her breathing grew swift and shallow and her eyes held a slumbrous, wondering quality, like a child waiting for Father Christmas.

She saw the flickering change of expressions on his face, ranging from a muscle-jerking tautness in his jaw to plain naked desire. Inch by inch he lowered his head and second by second she prepared herself for the explosive assault on her senses which she knew would follow. It was a dangerous situation, but somewhere along the line she had lost the will to resist. She wanted Warwick to kiss her more than anything else in the world.

It was not until his lips finally claimed hers that panic set in, but it was too late to back out. Already a flare of need had ignited inside her, and her arms crept traitorously around him.

Always of the opinion that no member of the opposite sex found her attractive, she had created a defensive wall which she hugged tightly around her on all occasions; but now a crack had appeared. She had been told she was frigid by her sister, that it was her standoffishness that put men off, but Libby had known it was nothing of the sort. Men simply saw nothing in her to appreciate.

That was why she felt so much more strongly now, why the emotions she had kept under wraps were flooding, out of control, to the surface. Paula and Rebecca were forgotten. Nothing mattered except the feel of this man's mouth on hers.

As he lifted his head to look at her she was shocked to see the hard glitter in his eyes. 'I warned you this day would come, Libby.'

'Whatever happens between us, you'll want it as much as me.' That's what he had said, and how right he was. Dear lord, how could she have forgotten? What a fool she was once more making of herself. This assault on her senses had been deliberate.

His mouth was back on hers before she could speak, a feather-light touch from which she could easily escape. How well he knew what she was feeling. He knew that his touch had triggered a response, that her heartbeats pattered like heavy rain on a tin roof, and that there was no way she could summon up the strength to resist him.

His lips moved to press light kisses on her eyelids, trailing slowly, oh, so slowly over her cheekbones, nibbling the lobe of her ear, and then descending to the arched column of her throat, seeking and finding the give-away, pounding pulse.

All the time Libby's fingers were involuntarily exploring, feeling the shape of his head and shoulders, the muscled strength in his back. Her heart was ruling her head, her mind warring with common sense, and heaven alone knew what was stopping her from putting an end to this deliberate assault on her senses!

The musky male scent of him was like a drug. His mouth moved with incredible erotic slowness to the hollow between her breasts, his tongue tasting the soft warmth of her skin, his hands pulling their hips hard together, making her shockingly aware of the intensity of his need.

Such intimate contact detonated through Libby like a firework, erupting into every nerve and tissue, leaving her feeling shaky and out of control, every bone melting, so that without even realising what she was doing she clung tightly to him.

'I could make love to you until you're begging for mercy,' he muttered, taking a nipple in his mouth, driving her half delirious with wanting. 'You're so refreshingly innocent.'

It was this pointed reminder of her naïveté that brought Libby to her senses. She forced open her heavy eyelids, blinking rapidly to clear the haze that clouded her vision, fighting to free herself, pushing at him with both hands. 'Stop it!' she gasped. 'Get away from me.'

'Libby.' He caught her wrists easily, and his voice was as thick with emotion as her own. 'Why deny yourself what you know you want?'

'I don't.' Fear pounded, and she twisted her face away, knowing how easily her emotions were reflected in her eyes. She dragged in a couple of steadying breaths as he let go of her hands.

'Liar; you're fooling no one.' Already he was master of himself, nothing in his voice now to suggest that only seconds ago he had been as dangerously close to losing control as she had, proving beyond any shadow of doubt that it was pure lust that had motivated him and nothing else.

Her blood chilling now in her veins, anger that she had made such a fool of herself giving her the strength she needed to face him coldly, Libby turned back, the sheet held tautly and defensively over her. 'Maybe you do have the power to make me lose my control, but only a swine would behave the way you do when he's engaged to be married to someone else.'

His affected innocence was laughable. 'What are you talking about, Libby?'

'You and Paula, of course; don't try to pretend that you didn't propose to her this morning—she told me so herself.' Libby's chin was high, her eyes a cold, pale amethyst; she was absolutely in control of herself now. 'Actually, I pity her. I wonder if she has any idea what you're really like. Perhaps I should tell her?'

'Feel free,' he suggested pleasantly.

'No, thanks; I'll let her find out for herself. Please leave my room.'

His mouth twisted wryly as he pushed himself lazily to his feet. 'You're even more beautiful when you're angry. Is it any wonder that I want you in my bed? I think the fates were kind when they sent you to me.'

Libby gasped at his audacity. 'Get out!'

'Is it because of Paula that you're unwilling to let me make love to you? Are you jealous of her?'

'"Jealous"?' she echoed scornfully. 'She's welcome to you—to every lousy, rotten inch. What would she say, do you think, if I told her I was actually your prisoner and not your employee? Do you think it would make any difference? Has she any idea that you have such a cruel streak?'

'I doubt she'd believe you,' he answered insouciantly. 'Paula thinks I can do no wrong; she's been infatuated with me ever since we first met.'

'Then why haven't you got married before now?'

'We each had our careers, which came before anything else,' he replied easily.

Everything he said was a confirmation of Paula's earlier statement. But such a marriage wouldn't work, she felt sure. Paula gave the impression of always putting herself first. There wouldn't be any give in their relationship—it would be all take, and at the end of the day Warwick would be a very unhappy man. Couldn't he see what she was like? Was he so blinded by love that he couldn't see she was the wrong type of woman for him?

But who was the right type? Someone like herself? Libby mentally and furiously shook her head. She was too much the other way. She was too soft, too inexperienced in the ways of the world, without the glamour he clearly favoured. She had been reasonably clever at school, but when her father had died and her mother become ill she had finished her schooling early to look after the home, doing a few hours a week at a local hairdresser's, and a course at the local college during the evenings, until she felt she was sufficiently experienced to set up on her own. Being a mobile hairdresser gave her the flexibility that she needed.

'And now is the right time to get married, is that what you're saying?' she asked sharply.

He shrugged. 'Paula thinks so.'

And he was not going to argue with her? Libby wondered why she felt so dispirited at the thought. It was crazy, she couldn't understand it, and more than anything in the world she wanted to be left alone. But there was the evening to be got through yet.

'Hurry now and get ready,' he said, as though reading her actual thoughts. 'Wear something nice—it's a classy place.' He had gone before she could answer.

Libby obeyed because it was a preferable alternative. His kiss had been nothing to what she could expect if they stayed here.

What had made her pack this one special dress, Libby did not know. She had only worn it once, at a friend's summer wedding, but it had seemed the right sort of thing for a hot climate, and so she had stuffed it into her case.

The deep lavender silk reflected the colour of her eyes, shoelace-thin straps left her shoulders bare and showed off her newly acquired tan, and the myriad tiny pleats in the skirt moved with sensuous rhythm as she walked. It was an essentially feminine dress, and she had the sudden thought that she was making a mistake wearing it—that it would further encourage Warwick's advances; but he was already calling out to her to make haste. It was too late to change into something safer.

Quickly now she brushed her hair and fastened it back in her nape with a lavender ribbon. She sprayed L'Aimant on her pulses and fixed silver filigree earrings to her ears and a silver chain about her wrist.

She ascended the short flight of steps into the saloon with a frantically beating heart, and she had to admit that Warwick looked magnificent in an ivory lightweight suit, with a sand-coloured shirt and an ivory tie. Much to her disgust, desire washed over her again. How could she feel like this when she hated him? How could she? Would there ever come a time when she could look at him and feel nothing? What sort of a person had he turned her into? He had awoken dormant feelings in her body, and now it seemed that she was never going to get rid of them. She had become as sensual as her sister, wanting a man for one reason only.

Her pulses throbbed as his eyes skimmed over her. He began with her eyes and mouth, then down the long, slender column of her neck and over the faint curve of her breasts. He paused there fractionally, as though reflecting on the way he had touched her so intimately earlier, then went down to her narrow waist and rounded hips, down the long length of her slender legs right to her feet in white high-heeled sandals. And then back up to her eyes again.

A muscle jerked tautly in his jaw. 'Let's go,' he rapped, and she had no idea whether he approved or not.

He gave her a helping hand off the boat and took her arm as they walked along the pontoon, heedful that her thin heels might get stuck in the space between the wooden slats. He unlocked a steel-blue Mercedes, and handed her into it, making sure she was sitting comfortably before closing the door.

By the time he had finished fussing, Libby's heart felt as though it were ready to burst out of her ribcage. She folded her hands demurely in her lap and tried to look cool and uninterested as he climbed in beside her. But surely he could hear her heart? It was so loud it echoed inside her head, blotting out all other sounds.

The car was air-conditioned and yet Libby felt uncomfortably warm; it was spacious and yet she felt it wrapping itself around her, drawing Warwick closer and closer until she felt that she was being consumed by him. She could no longer smell her own perfume; she was aware only of the strong musky scent of him that incited every one of her senses. Was this what he had set out to do?

She found herself wanting to reach out and touch him, wanting to turn her head and look at him, wanting to press her lips to his skin and taste him. They were feelings that had never been a part of her life until now, and she would have scorned anyone who dared to suggest that she would experience such emotions. But they were so strong! And it was this man who had awoken them!

How was she going to get through the evening without making an even bigger fool of herself? She had never found it easy to hide her emotions—sadness, anger, happiness, they all showed. Could he tell that she was

aroused beyond measure? That there was a danger of
its cancelling out her hatred? Or was this his aim? Was
this what it was all about? He wanted her to be like putty
in his hands so that he could do what he liked with her.
What was it he had said? 'You're mine in every sense
of the word.' A shiver ran down her spine.

The restaurant was on the outskirts of Torviscas, in
an enviable position above the bay, and they were the
first ones there. They sat outside on a long, wide balcony
that was sheltered from the winds that blew frequently
in the islands, with a screen of brilliantly hued
bougainvillaea and sweet-scented honeysuckle, grown in
tubs and trained over wooden lattice-work.

A moon hung full and pendulous above them in a
star-strewn sky. It was a warm, scented night—a night
for romance, thought Libby, a night for lovers. So what
was she doing here? She felt cold now, cold and afraid,
not so much of Warwick but of the feelings he was in-
ducing inside her.

He had helped her out of the car, and his touch had
seared her skin like a branding-iron. Along the short path
to the restaurant she had kept a deliberate distance between them, but again as she sat down he had forestalled
an attentive waiter and held out her chair, not moving
until she was comfortable. And this was only the beginning! It was going to be a difficult night.

'This is a nice place,' she murmured, realising she must
say something to break the tension that was in danger
of building to breaking-point. 'Or is that traitorous?'
she added with an impish smile. The green-painted tables
were covered with pink linen cloths, candles sat inside
squat green bottles. It had a garden air to it—a well-
kept garden. Pretty little lights hung like glow-worms
from invisible wires, and hauntingly soft music played
in the background.

'It's traitorous,' he grunted. 'We'll see what the food's like.'

She could tell that he too begrudgingly liked what he saw. Perhaps he did not like to think that there were better places than his own? 'Tell me about your restaurants,' she said. 'How many have you got?'

'Four,' he replied willingly. 'Two here in Tenerife, one in Lanzarote, one in Gran Canaria.'

'Do you plan to open any more?'

'I don't think so.'

'What made you decide to be a restaurateur?'

His eyes narrowed. 'So many questions.'

Libby shrugged. 'You know all about me, why shouldn't I ask about you?' She knew nothing except that he was very rich and had a hard streak to him that wasn't at first noticeable.

'There is a difference,' he pointed out sardonically, 'but if you're really interested, then I'll tell you. Stop me if you get bored.'

'I won't,' she answered confidently.

'When I first left school I was a no-hoper. I had no idea what I wanted to do, drifting from one job to another until eventually I decided I'd like to be a chef. My parents were disappointed in me, I know. They'd had such high hopes.'

'Were you an only child?'

He nodded. 'I was born late in my parents' life, and I suppose I was indulged, as they'd given up all hope of ever having children. With this new ambition I went to college during the day on a catering course, and took a job as a bartender in the evenings. I've never been afraid of hard work, you understand, it's just that I had no particular aim.'

He sounded a bit like Rebecca, thought Libby wryly.

'On my twenty-first birthday my parents took me out for a meal in the West End. When I saw the prices they were charging I realised there was more money to be made in owning a place like that than working in one. From that moment my mind was made up.'

'But how did you get the money?' frowned Libby. 'It costs thousands to set up a place such as this. And why did you choose here instead of England?'

He lifted his shoulders carelessly. 'I came out here for—well, personal reasons. I needed to get away from England—nothing to do with my parents,' he assured her. 'I love them dearly and still visit them as often as I can. But here seemed a good place—sunshine all the year round, tourists all the year round, nothing seasonal.'

'So you did your homework? You didn't pick the Canary Islands willy-nilly?'

'Heavens, no. It was all carefully worked out in my mind beforehand. When I first came here I worked in bars and restaurants, saving every penny, living as cheaply as I could, until finally I was able to open El Terraplén, here in Torviscas. It wasn't as plush as it is now, but it was a start. The rest followed. It's been hard work, but now it's paying off—and that's enough about me. Let's make the most of tonight. An aperitif to start with, I think. A dry sherry. Tio Pepe, perhaps?'

Libby was disappointed he had stopped. She was interested in everything he had to say. It was difficult to believe that he had once been a man without ambition. He had achieved so much in a short space of time.

When the sherry came he lifted his glass. *'Salud!'*

Libby smiled back. *'Salud!'* And sipped the pale liquid carefully. She had only nibbled at her chicken at lunchtime, and did not want the sherry to go to her head. It was very important that she kept her wits about her. Warwick would want to kiss her again, she knew, but she was equally determined that it should not happen. It was proving far too easy to lose her head.

The tables were beginning to fill up, and the hum of conversation successfully isolated them. Before, the balcony had seemed large and impersonal; now they were in their own little space, and she felt that she was breathing him in again. It was far too intimate. She studied the leather-bound menu and tried to pretend he wasn't there.

'Do you know that your eyes in the candle-light look like lavender blossom with the morning dew still upon them?' His tone was deliberately soft and sensual, sliding silkily along her nerve-streams like a ten-year-old brandy.

Despite her good intentions, Libby began to glow. Whatever bad points he had, there was no doubt that he knew how to make a woman feel good.

Far below them the harbour lights twinkled. The *Estoque* was indiscernible from this distance, but they would be going back to it afterwards, and she could not help but feel a tautness inside her at the thought.

The food was truly excellent, and Warwick attentive, almost lover-like. It was impossible to tell that she was his prisoner, or that she was a useful diversion in Paula's absence! To an outsider it would look as though she meant more to him than anyone else in the world.

'A penny for them.'

Libby hadn't realised that she had lapsed into silence. 'They're not worth it.'

'I presume that I figured in them?'

She shrugged. 'Among other things.'

'Paula?'

'Maybe.'

'Your sister?'

'Of course. How long do you intend keeping me here?'
It was far better to bring up an inflammatory subject
than sit here worrying about her wanton feelings.

'Probably several weeks,' he said easily.

Libby looked at him, horror-stricken. 'You have to be
joking! You can't do that. I refuse to stay.'

'You have no choice, Libby. You'll go when I'm ready
to let you go. Why are you spoiling such a lovely
evening?' His hand touched hers across the table, trig-
gering off an electrifying response, and for several long
seconds his eyes held hers. 'Let's get out of here,' he
muttered thickly, making no attempt to hide his blatant
desire.

Libby tried to demur, but it made no difference, and
she knew that the moment they got back to the *Estoque*
he would want to make love to her. Would she have the
strength to resist?

But, surprisingly, he drove up into the hills and
through tiny villages well off the beaten track. It looked
as though she had misjudged him, and gradually she relaxed. Soon they were descending, down, down, down
until they came to a tiny bay hemmed in all around by
the hills.

'Very few tourists find their way here,' he told her.

They got out of his car and scrambled down the last
few yards to a pocket-handkerchief beach of coarse dark
sand. Libby could see everything clearly in the light from
the moon, boulders tumbling into the sea on either side
of them, waves lapping the wind-rippled sand, bushes
and scrub hanging tenaciously to the hillside.

It had a raw kind of beauty that appealed to her, but
she was more conscious of Warwick at her side than
anything else. 'Do you like it?' His tone throbbed low
and sensual close to her ear, closer than she had thought,
and goose-bumps rose on her skin.

She did not answer—she could not bring herself to speak; instead she nodded, and it seemed the most natural thing in the world when he put his arm about her shoulders and they walked to the water's edge.

The Atlantic Ocean was tame in this protected corner of the island, black as ink, each wave, each ripple tipped with silver, and as they stood there in the warm night air Warwick said, 'The water looks inviting.'

She nodded, feeling the heat from his body, an almost impossible heat that flooded through her limbs as though he were pouring it into her, combining with her own warmth, together making her feel as though she were on fire.

'Shall we?' he challenged, his eyes black in the moonlight but no less potent, and Libby felt him drugging her senses.

Skinny-dipping in the moonlight? Dared she do such a thing? It would be so unlike her. But already her heart was thudding wildly at the thought of it. It would be dangerously exciting with Warwick in the mood he was in. On the other hand, perhaps the cold water would cool his ardour? Perhaps that was why he had suggested it?

It crossed her mind that at this moment in time she no longer hated him. The loving feelings she had experienced on the plane had returned—with a vengeance! It was insanity, when she knew they were not returned, when she knew it was all some game he was playing. It amused him to have her wanting him. She was a toy to be played with until such time as he deemed that retribution had been paid. So why was she going along with it?

'What are you afraid of, Libby?'

The taunting tone in his voice made her lift her chin. 'Who says I'm afraid?'

'Then why are you taking so long to make up your mind?'

'I didn't realise I was,' she lied. 'It's an excellent idea.' Her reply was no louder than a breath of wind, her eyes held to his by a force stronger than anything she had ever experienced.

'Then let me help you get undressed.' Libby wanted to object, but already he was undoing the ribbon in her hair, and in that one tiny act there was an intimacy that could not have been created by anyone else but Warwick. It took every ounce of self-control to stand still and not turn into his arms. It was idiotic, but just having him so close drugged her senses to such an extent that all sane reasoning fled.

With excruciating slowness he slid the straps from her shoulders, his fingers scorching her skin, all the time his eyes locked into hers. He turned her around, gently, oh, so gently, and unzipped her dress, not letting it fall to the sand but pulling it down carefully.

Libby heard his swift intake of breath as her naked breasts were exposed, but she could not believe that he hadn't known how she was dressed. Men noticed that sort of thing. She'd really had no choice, as she had forgotten to pack a strapless bra.

Her nipples were erect, her breasts hard and aching for his touch, and to her amazement she felt no embarrassment. He did not touch her; he carried on removing her dress, steadying her as she stepped out of it, folding it carefully and placing it on a smooth, flat rock.

'The moonlight enhances your beauty, Libby.' There was an unsteady tremor to his voice. 'You look almost immortal, like a goddess—Venus, perhaps—born of the foam of the sea.'

He began to undress himself. His hard-muscled chest looked like polished teak in the moonlight, his stomach was taut and flat, his legs long and powerful. He was all man, a strong, virile man, and she was in danger of losing her heart to him!

When he began to pull off his tight black briefs she turned away, heard his soft chuckle, then the next second felt his hands on her hips, his fingers slipping into her own scrap of silk, easing it down until she too was completely naked.

His touch had been that of a gentleman, she could not accuse him of assaulting her, and yet she felt ravaged, her whole body on fire and aching, aching desperately with need for him. She fled quickly towards the water, knowing that if she stood there any longer she would offer herself to him—and that would be fatal.

She heard his sudden exclamation and his laughter as he followed, and she splashed through the shallows, quickening her steps, launching herself into the deeper water.

It was not as cold as she had imagined, and Warwick was close behind her. He swam like a fish, skimming through the water, propelling himself beneath her and surfacing suddenly in front of her.

She laughed with the sheer joy of it all. They stood on the sandy bottom, and the water came up to Libby's breasts. He put his hands on her waist and lifted her, letting her slide down his body, the water silken smooth between them, his eyes meeting and locking into hers.

She felt inflamed by him, excited beyond all measure. His arms bound her to him, and he covered her mouth with his, his lips cool and firm and demanding.

It was insanity! Libby twisted herself free with a teasing laugh, swimming away from him, knowing he could catch her easily if he wanted to. They played like porpoises, surfacing and diving, swimming around each other, their bodies gliding together, his hands touching her so lightly that she wondered whether it was imagination. It was the most erotic experience of Libby's life.

All too soon Warwick said that they'd had enough, and they swam back to the shore together, Warwick keeping pace with her, his arm around her waist as they found their feet in shallower water.

A few yards up the shore he pulled her close, two cool bodies touching and inciting, and involuntarily Libby's arms slid around him, feeling the movement of hard muscle beneath wet silken skin.

Tingles of warmth began to creep through her veins as Warwick held her, his hands sliding up and down the gentle curve of her back, an erotic touch, a touch that pulsed with meaning, with need.

Without realising what she was doing, Libby urged herself against him, hip against hip, thigh against thigh. Never in her life had she felt so wanton.

Warwick pushed her gently, ever so gently from him, a question in his eyes, asking her without words whether she knew what she was doing. In response Libby lifted her mouth to his. With a groan his arms tightened around her and his lips crushed hers in a kiss that was deep and spine-tingling, his tongue entering the moist cavern of her mouth. Libby felt herself melting, and clung hard to him as she became boneless.

One hand reached up to caress her nape beneath the wet fall of her hair and the delicate, sensitive skin behind her ear, trailing with searing, feather-light touches to her shoulder, then creeping downwards to worship the soft mound of her breasts.

With aching slowness he traced her outline, stroking, stimulating, arousing, taking all the time in the world to reach her nipple, finally holding it between thumb and forefinger. Squeezing, pulling, tormenting, until she felt that she was slowly going out of her mind.

She closed her eyes and let her head fall back. His
other hand was in the small of her back, her hips still
held firmly against his, and she could feel his arousal,
and it affected her deeply.

Her breathing grew erratic, her mouth dry, and when
he lowered his head and sucked her cool, damp nipple
into his mouth she felt as though she was going to faint.
No one had ever prepared her for such exquisite pleasure.
It pulsed through every corner of her body. She arched
her back and curled her toes in the sand, and his name
fell from her lips. 'Warwick, oh, Warwick!'

His hand moved down her body, burning her, making
its way slowly, indescribably slowly to the very heart of
her, and somewhere in the mist of her passion Libby
knew she had to put a stop to it. If she let him make
love to her she would bitterly regret it for the rest of her
life. She wrenched herself free and turned her back on
him, her shoulders hunched, her fingers clenched into
fists against her mouth, and she felt herself shaking in
every limb.

'Libby, have I hurt you?' Warwick's hand touched
her shoulder and swung her gently to face him.

'No.' She tried to make her tone crisp and decisive,
but ended up sounding miserable.

'Then what the hell——?'

His sudden anger made her eyes flash in self-defence.
'I came to my senses.' Her voice was stronger now. 'You
had no right trying to take advantage of me.'

'"Take advantage"?' he snarled. 'You were as eager
as me; deny it if you can!'

'I can't deny it,' she admitted shamefully. 'I can only
be thankful that common sense saved me from doing
something I know I would have lived to regret. You're
a real swine, Warwick Hunter. You think nothing of
taking a woman just for the sheer hell of it.'

His lips compressed grimly. 'I think it's time we went.'

There were no gentle helping hands this time to help her get dressed, and pulling on a silk dress over damp skin was not easy. Warwick was ready long before her, and impatiently he said, 'Here, let me,' when she struggled to pull up her zip.

He was careful not to touch her, but it made no difference—his nearness was just as fatal. Libby tensed herself, holding her breath, not letting it go until he moved away, and then, with her shoes in her hand, she followed him up the short rocky incline to his car.

She expected him to drive straight back to the boat, but he didn't. He drove fast for seemingly endless miles, silent, face grim. Was he angry with her, she wondered, or with himself for wanting to make love to her in the first place? It was a pity she had needed to put an end to such powerful emotions. But it was for the best. She would never have been able to live with herself if she had gone through with it.

Gradually his fingers became less tense on the wheel, and he did not drive as though all the hounds in hell were after him. He glanced at her once, but she did not meet his eyes, and he swung the car around in an arc and headed back the way they had come.

CHAPTER SIX

NOT surprisingly, after her disastrous night out Libby had difficulty in sleeping. She had gone to bed the moment they had got home without saying another word to Warwick. She was far too embarrassed. She ought never to have let things go as far as they had. What madness had possessed her? Why had she gone swimming in the nude? Why had she gone swimming at all? Never in her life had she done anything so impulsive or so crazy.

Was it any wonder that Warwick had got the wrong impression? Yet it had been impossible to resist him. It was so easy to forget that he was her captor, that he was intent on exacting his own form of revenge. Even making love to her was part of the punishment. So why hadn't she realised that? Why had she pushed everything else out of her mind except the fact that he was the most charismatic man she had ever met?

The only thing she could be thankful for was that he had not forced himself on her. Even though he was angry he had deferred to her wishes—for now! She couldn't be sure that he wouldn't try to make love to her again; in fact it was a stone-cold certainty that he would. She was his in every sense of the word, that was what he had claimed, and she had no doubt that Warwick Hunter always meant what he said.

The next morning Libby deliberately did not rise early, even though she was awake at dawn. She wanted to give Warwick time to eat his breakfast and go into his office. She wanted no further confrontation with him.

It was a futile exercise. Warwick was sitting in the saloon with an empty mug at his side and a newspaper in his hand. When she poured her own coffee and spread jam and butter on to a roll he joined her in the dinette.

'I was beginning to think that you weren't going to show your face. Are you trying to avoid me, Elizabeth?' His damp black hair curled crisply and his pungent aftershave sharply assailed her nostrils. He wore a white cotton T-shirt which emphasised his breadth of shoulder and the muscular hardness of his chest and biceps. Libby had never been more aware of his sensuality.

Beneath the table their knees were millimetres away from each other, and she deliberately tucked her legs under her seat. She wanted no contact whatsoever. Looking at him was bad enough. It puzzled her how she could feel like this about a man who had no compunction about using her. But at least she was still in his bad books. That was something. It would ensure he kept his distance. 'The simple answer is that I overslept,' she lied.

Thick brows rose sceptically. 'I assumed you wouldn't sleep at all. Obviously I was wrong in thinking that you had a conscience.'

'Obviously,' she agreed, needlessly stirring her coffee, doing anything rather than look at him.

'I have to go out for a couple of hours this morning,' he said, much to her surprise. 'Can I trust you to stay here?'

'Without my passport I'm hardly likely to go running anywhere, am I?' Her tone was filled with scorn.

'I'm glad you have more sense than to go against me.' His smoky eyes were hard and cold, as though last night had never happened. 'I'll try not to be long. Meanwhile the boat needs hosing down; I think that might keep you busy for an hour or two.'

Libby compressed her lips. He was most definitely mistaken if he thought he was going to use her as a galley-slave. He might think he had her in the palm of his hand, but nothing was further from the truth. She was still a free agent, even if she couldn't go back to England.

He watched the flush of anger creep up her neck to her cheeks, and with an abrupt change of subject said, 'You really were very beautiful in the moonlight. It was a pity the evening came to such an unfortunate end.'

'It should never have happened,' she retorted sharply.

'You had no reservations—to begin with,' he reminded her.

Libby tossed her head. 'That was a fatal mistake, but you can rest assured it won't happen again. I've learned my lesson.' She refused to look at him as she spoke, knowing that if she dared do so he would see in her eyes that she was not as immune to him as she was trying to make out. She was in an impossible situation, half hating, half loving him, feeling drugged with his nearness, with the maddening, sensual scent of him.

'That's a pity,' he said softly. 'It was a most enjoyable experience—for both of us, I'm sure—and one I have every intention of repeating.'

Libby looked at him sharply. 'Oh, no, I shall never be so foolish again.'

He smiled humourlessly. 'We'll see.' And then, with another of his sudden subject changes, 'By the way, I'm holding a party tomorrow night.'

'A party?' asked Libby, stunned. 'How can you think about entertaining when Rebecca is missing? You should be doing something about looking for her instead of organising a party.'

'My life doesn't revolve around your sister,' he told her harshly.

Libby supposed he was right, but she hoped he wasn't expecting her to be a part of it. Celebrating was the last thing she felt like doing. 'Will Paula be coming?'

'No.' He didn't look disappointed. 'As far as I know she'll still be in Madrid. You'll be my partner for the evening, Libby.'

Her heart thudded, but at the same time she looked at him derisively. 'I thought I was your prisoner? Besides, what will people think, seeing a complete stranger?'

'That I'm very lucky to have such a gorgeous girl living on my boat.'

'Gorgeous'? Libby knew he had to be lying. Gorgeous was the last word she would use to describe herself. But she was beginning to realise that Warwick always used flattery to get what he wanted. 'Aren't you forgetting that you're engaged to Paula?' she asked coldly.

'No one knows,' he reminded her.

Libby knew she was fighting a losing battle and that she might as well make the most of a bad job, even though it seemed the wrong thing to be doing at this moment in time. 'So what are you doing about food?' She assumed he would want her to prepare it.

'It's all taken care of,' he replied with a smile. 'All you need do is make yourself look beautiful.'

Less than a week ago Libby would have laughed if anyone had said that to her. Now she knew it wasn't such an impossibility. Every day her reflection in the mirror told her that she was blossoming. There was a glow about her that was new. She looked a different girl—and all because of Warwick—because of these feelings that unwittingly filled her body when he was around. Most of the time it was impossible to hate him, even though she knew it was what she ought to be feeling.

'What sort of people will be attending?' she asked, trying to shake off these unwanted thoughts.

'Friends, colleagues, business acquaintances. Wear that little purple dress you had on the other night. You looked ravishing in that.'

Painful memories flooded back, and Libby's cheeks burned. She would never wear that dress again. It was bundled in a bag at the bottom of her wardrobe, out of sight, but not, unfortunately, out of mind. 'I'll see,' she murmured, privately deciding to wear something more demure.

She wanted no repeat of what had happened at the beach. Not that she blamed Warwick entirely. She had been as guilty as he of wanting to make love. But it was the first and last time. She would steer clear in future of any unhealthy situations. He really was a rat, and it was obvious his commitment to Paula didn't mean a thing. Would he remain faithful after they were married? she wondered.

Once breakfast was cleared away and Warwick had left, Libby went for a walk around the marina. She always enjoyed looking at the other boats. The *Sea Eagle* was a catamaran owned by a giant of a Scotsman of about Warwick's age, with coarse corn-coloured hair and a cheerful smile. Yesterday he had tried to hold Libby in conversation, introducing himself as Iain McTaggart, but she had simply smiled and walked on her way. This morning, however, he seemed determined to talk to her.

'Lassie, why is it that you look so sad?' He had jumped off his boat when he'd seen her coming, and now stood barring her way.

'Do I?' asked Libby in surprise.

'Without a doubt,' he told her firmly. 'I take it you're not here on holiday?'

She shook her head. 'No, I'm not.'

'Is Warwick Hunter your boyfriend?' As he spoke he glanced across at the *Estoque*.

She allowed herself a faint smile. 'No, I'm simply waiting for my sister, Rebecca Eaton. She used to work for Warwick. Do you know her?'

'I remember a girl, yes, but I doubt she was a relative of yours. A brassy blonde, thought she was a glamour-puss, but only succeeded in making herself look cheap. Got her eye on anything in trousers—tried to chat me up once. I sent her on her way. I prefer to do my own chasing.'

'That's my sister,' confirmed Libby grimly.

'Oh, lord! I'm sorry.' To her amazement he looked embarrassed. 'I shouldn't have said all that.'

'Don't apologise,' she grimaced. 'I know what she's like. Have you seen her recently? I seem to have missed her.'

'Afraid I can't help you there, lassie. She hasn't been around for a week or more. Maybe she'll come back; I don't know. How long are you planning on waiting? Perhaps I could take you out and show you around the island? I've noticed you never seem to go anywhere.'

'You're very kind,' said Libby, 'and thanks, but no thanks.' He was also a bit cheeky, but she liked him for it. It made a change speaking to someone other than Warwick. She wondered if anyone else had noticed that she never strayed far from the boat. Even so, they would never guess that she'd had her passport confiscated and was a virtual prisoner.

An excursion, however, was exactly what she needed, and she was glad the Scotsman had put the idea into her mind. She would go now, today, if possible. It would serve two purposes: she would see more of Tenerife, and she could look out for her sister at the same time.

Excitement mounting, she fetched her bag from the boat and made her way to the hotel where she had stayed the first night. She had seen a whole list of trips advertised there, and to her delight she discovered that a coach was leaving in a little over an hour's time for Mount Teide.

If Warwick came back while she was away it would do him good to worry about her, thought Libby gleefully. And it was certainly better than washing down his boat.

The coach was full, and they were a friendly crowd, most of them English although there were a few Germans and Scandinavians. The road climbed gradually, and a few hundred feet above sea-level the barren scenery changed. They passed through a forest of pines and lush green vegetation, but all too soon it turned to stratified volcanic lava where only scrub clung tenaciously to the mountain sides. Every now and then they caught sight of the snow-capped tip of Mount Teide, but it always seemed elusively distant until, after winding round and round and up and up, they were finally there.

The air was clear and cold and the snow on the mountain-side frozen solid. Libby was glad she had been told to take a jacket with her. A cable-car took them up the last few hundred feet of this highest mountain in Spain, and Libby exulted in the feeling of being suspended in space. Although the volcano was reputedly dormant she could still smell the sulphur, and her feeling of excitement increased.

It was a clear day and bitterly cold so high up, and there were perfect panoramic views all around of Tenerife, of the other islands, and she wouldn't have been surprised to see Africa itself. Amazingly, she wished Warwick were here with her. The courier churned out information, but Libby would have preferred to hear it from Warwick. His sensual voice would have sent shivers down her spine, and maybe she would not have heard all that he said, or indeed any of it!

She disappointingly saw nothing of Rebecca, even though she kept a sharp lookout at all times. Not that she actually expected to find her sister in a place like this, but there was always a chance, and at least she felt she was doing something.

It was dusk when she got back, and the boat was in darkness, but as she walked along the pontoon and stepped on to the *Estoque* Warwick appeared out of nowhere. 'Where the devil have you been?' He looked angry enough to explode.

On the tip of her tongue to tell him, Libby suddenly changed her mind. He wasn't her keeper. Why should he question her movements like this? Why shouldn't she be allowed to go out? He knew she would come back again. 'I don't see that it's any business of yours,' she said defiantly.

'I think it is my business,' he retorted.

'You don't own me,' she tossed back, 'even though you like to think you do.' He was spoiling the day for her, taking all the pleasure out of it.

'At the moment you are my responsibility, and I think I have every right to know where you've been.'

'*Your* responsibility?' she countered heatedly. 'We both know the reason I'm here, and it doesn't give you any say over what I do. If I want to go out I'll go, and I don't have to answer to you.'

He snorted savagely, his eyes hard, and, taking hold of her wrist, he dragged her inside, flicking on the light and looking at her coldly. 'I'm waiting, Libby.'

She tilted her chin. 'If you must know, I've been to Mount Teide.' She ought to have known he would squeeze the information out of her one way or another.

'I thought it a pity to go home and see nothing of the island.'

His eyes narrowed suspiciously. 'And who accompanied you on this trip?'

Her brows rose. 'I went by myself, of course. I'm not actually overwhelmed with friends.'

'Are you saying you haven't been with that Scottish bastard with the catamaran?'

He actually sounded jealous, though Libby knew this couldn't be true. 'What would happen if I said I had?'

'Then I wouldn't like to be in his shoes,' he growled.

'He's a big man, Warwick,' she pointed out, her lips quirking. 'But actually, no, I haven't been with him. I went on a coach trip all by myself. Satisfied?'

Still he scowled. 'I saw you talking to him this morning.'

Libby frowned. Surely Warwick had left the marina by the time she took her walk? Had he been spying on her? Was he watching her every movement even when she thought him safely out of sight? The thought left a nasty taste in her mouth.

'What was he saying to you?'

Her eyes flashed, her chin lifted, his behaviour infuriating her. 'He wanted to know why I looked so sad. I told him it was because I was being kept prisoner against my will, and that if I dared go out of sight you'd be after me with a meat-cleaver.'

Warwick snorted angrily. 'Very funny. Now what were you really talking about?'

Libby shrugged, the fight going out of her. 'He did ask why I looked sad. I told him about Rebecca being missing—but not,' she added quickly, 'that she had stolen some money.'

'Afraid that it might reflect on you?' he sneered, though he still did not look too sure whether he believed her or not. 'I would have taken you to Mount Teide myself if you'd asked.'

Libby threw him a sceptical look. 'Let's face it, I'm here as your prisoner, nothing more. Last night was enough of a disaster for neither of us to want to repeat the experiment. I enjoyed my own company, thank you very much, and now I'm going to take a shower. Excuse me.'

But he was not finished with her yet. 'The least you could have done was left a note,' he lashed out cruelly. 'I came back earlier than expected, and hoped to spend a few hours cruising.'

'So why didn't you?' she spat back, though her heart-beats suddenly accelerated at the thought he might have been seeking her company.

'I could hardly leave not knowing where you were.'

'So you drew the conclusion that I was out with Iain McTaggart?'

'He was nowhere in sight.'

'As a matter of fact,' she told him coldly, 'he did ask if he could take me out.'

She was unprepared for his tight-lipped anger, the fury that darkened his eyes. 'So I was right,' he snarled, 'Iain was chatting you up?'

'I really don't see that it has anything to do with you,' she answered, wanting to hurt him as he was hurting her. It would do him good to have his ego deflated. 'As a matter of fact I was very tempted.'

'So what stopped you?' His nostrils flared as he advanced on her, and his fingers curled into fists. There was something menacing about his whole stance that made Libby want to dash from the room. But pride forbade her.

'I hardly know the man.'

'You didn't know me when you decided to stay on my boat,' he pointed out.

But there was a whole world of difference. The Scotsman did nothing for her. She had fallen painfully in love with Warwick at first sight, and even the way he was treating her now made very little difference. 'I was waiting for my sister,' she reminded him. 'You told me she'd be back before morning. If I'd known you were lying, if I'd known she'd already gone missing, if I'd known what you were planning, I'd never have agreed to your suggestion.'

'The fact that you were—er—attracted to me had nothing to do with it?' he taunted.

Libby gasped. 'Nothing at all.' Her eyes were a bright, violent purple, her chin jutting defensively. 'You're a conceited swine if you think that. How could I be attracted to someone like you?'

'I think you're deluding yourself. I think we both know that the attraction was there instantly.'

'I think we both know that it was deliberate on your part,' she flung back. 'You had one aim in mind when you sat beside me on that plane.'

'Yes, I did,' he admitted, 'but we're not talking about my feelings, we're talking about yours.'

'You want to know how I feel?' she asked icily. 'Well, I'll tell you. I hate your guts. Is that blunt enough? And I'm looking forward to the day I can get out of here!'

A muscle jerked in his jaw and he looked at her for several long seconds, his eyes narrowed as though trying to assess whether she was speaking the truth.

Libby looked coldly back. In that moment she really did hate him. But why did he look as though he did not want to believe her? Heavens, she had every reason to feel as she did. How could he possibly expect her to feel otherwise? Did he think he was so irresistible that she would ignore little details like the fact that she was being kept here against her will?

To her relief he suddenly turned away and headed for his state-room. Libby went to her own cabin and showered and changed into one of her simple home-made cotton dresses.

Although it was dark it was too early to go to bed, and besides she was hungry as she had eaten nothing since breakfast. Oddly, she hadn't even thought about food, and yet now she was ravenous. To cook something would take too long, she decided, so instead she made herself a ham and tomato sandwich, and curled up in the saloon with her plate and a magazine. There was still no sign of Warwick.

But her sleepless night had taken its toll, and before Libby knew it her eyes closed, the magazine slipped from her fingers, and she knew nothing more until she felt Warwick's arms around her.

Instinctively she began to struggle. 'What the hell are you doing? Let me go!'

'I'm taking you to bed.' He had one arm under her knees, the other about her shoulders.

Her eyes flew wide, and she fought more strongly, instantly wide awake. 'Oh, no, you're not!' What insanity was taking hold of him? Did he think he could take up where he had left off yesterday?

'To your own bed, Libby, stop fighting me,' he growled. 'You were dead to the world and looked most uncomfortable.'

Feeling faintly foolish, Libby stilled her flailing arms. 'It's all right, I'm awake now, I can walk. I must have been more tired than I realised.'

But he did not let her go, and contact with him was explosive. Libby had to fight the urge to throw her arms around his neck and cling to him. The feel of his body next to hers was intoxicating and exciting, and when he put her down on the bed she did not want him to let her go. But she kept her feelings to herself, still glaring at him, her whole body stiff with rejection. He got the message, and left, tight-lipped, without saying another word.

It was impossible to sleep now. The sensation of Warwick's arms about her was still too vivid, the musky male scent of him lingered in her nostrils, and she could not help but wonder what would have happened if she'd gone along with her feelings instead of putting on a cold front.

Eventually she did fall asleep, but only to dream about Warwick, dream that they were living together on the boat in love and happiness, and she awoke the next morning with his name on her lips. It was going to be hard leaving him when the time came. Despite all her claims of hatred she actually did love him. And the fact that she knew she was a fool for doing so made no difference—even the fact that he was engaged to another girl.

It was an immense relief to find the boat silent and empty. She ate a leisurely breakfast of croissants—Warwick had a fresh supply of bread and vegetables delivered daily—and drank several cups of coffee before beginning the task of cleaning and tidying, making sure everything was spotless for the party. She even swabbed down the decks after all, and coiled the ropes back in their neat little circles.

'Ahoy there!'

It was late afternoon and she was on the upper deck lying in the sun. All the work was done, but she was still too much on edge to relax properly. At the sound of the Scottish voice she walked to the rail and looked down. The bluff blond man was standing on the walkway.

'What happened to you yesterday afternoon? I was looking for you.'

'I went to Mount Teide,' she confessed with a smile.

'Not with Warwick Hunter, I saw him here.'

'On my own, actually.'

'And yet you turned me down,' he accused sadly.

'I'm sorry.'

'What you're trying to say politely is that I'm not your type?' There was a rueful twist to his lips as he spoke. 'Perhaps you have a boyfriend back home, is that it?'

'No, there's no one,' admitted Libby.

'It's a pity, a great pity; you're a bonny wee lass, and no mistake. If you should ever change your mind you know where I am. Is there any news of your sister?'

Libby shook her head. 'Not yet. I fear I'm wasting my time.'

'You're not thinking of leaving?' He looked truly upset at the thought. 'The place wouldn't be the same without you. I look forward to seeing you walking around the marina. You truly brighten my day. Would you like to come to my boat for a drink?'

'No, she damn well would not!'

Libby had not seen Warwick return, and now she looked on horrified as he caught hold of the other man's shoulder and seemed prepared to punch him in the face.

Iain McTaggart pulled sharply away. 'You lay another finger on me, mate, and you'll be sorry. I'll go, but only because I don't want to upset this lovely lassie by causing a scene.' He looked up at Libby and gave a tight smile. 'The offer's still there whenever you feel like it.' He brushed past Warwick without even looking at him.

Libby moved away from the rail, feeling sorry for the other man, and angry with Warwick for reacting so violently. In two seconds he was at her side. 'What the hell was all that about?' His eyes were cold and grey and furious, and he was breathing heavily.

'We were only talking,' Libby defended. 'He was doing no harm. You had no right speaking to him like that.'

'I'll speak how I damn well like!' he rapped grimly. 'I know exactly what he was doing.'

'You think I'd have gone on his boat?' she flashed.

'You looked mighty friendly to me.'

'You're insane! What are you afraid of, that he might help me to get back to England? That he has a nice little business forging false passports? Or knows someone who can? You make me sick, Warwick, but the truth of the matter is that if I'd wanted to go you wouldn't have been able to stop me.'

'You underestimate me,' he ground out, his hands clenched into fists at his side. 'While you're with me I want you associating with no other man.'

Libby walked to the other side of the deck before turning to face him again, her hands on the metal rail behind her. 'You're an arrogant swine, Warwick Hunter.'

'And you hate me, yes, I know.' His cool, unnerving smile froze the blood in her veins. 'But my word is law around here, and you'd better believe it. I make a good friend but a dangerous enemy. If you think I'm evil now, then try defying me and find out what I'm like!'

Libby had no doubt that he was speaking the truth, and she had no intention of doing anything heroic; incurring his wrath would be like splitting open hell. But she did not see why she should not be free to choose her own friends. What harm was she doing speaking to the jolly Scotsman?

A white delivery van driving slowly along the marina caught Warwick's attention, and he swung himself down on to the ladder and leapt off the boat. The food for the party had arrived.

Not only food, but also drinks and fresh flowers, and Libby spent the next hour sorting and arranging. As soon as she had finished she went to her cabin and stayed there until it was time to get ready.

Not wanting to let Warwick down by wearing anything home-made, Libby decided on one of the dresses that Rebecca had left behind. In cream silk jersey, it had a vest-type top and the skirt was ribbed so that it looked as though it fell in a series of pleats, the whole pulled together with a wide gilt belt. It skimmed her curves but did not blatantly define them, and Libby felt reasonably safe in it.

Until Warwick looked at her! Leaving the sanctity of her cabin, she ventured up into the saloon, and found him already there. He wore white trousers and shirt and a black bow-tie, and was more handsome than ever. But it was his eyes on her that were the most disturbing.

Libby had seen nothing the least sensual in the dress she had chosen. Looking at her reflection carefully in the mirror, she had reassured herself that she did not look as attractive as she had in the lavender silk, had decided there was nothing at all in her appearance to encourage Warwick's advances.

His eyes narrowed upon her, seeming to see the woman underneath rather than the clothing which covered her. It was a long, slow, heart-stopping appraisal, and Libby felt every inch as aroused as she had that night on the beach. The evening was going to be agony, she knew it already—a complete disaster. He was going to play the game of finding her attractive all over again.

'I asked you to wear your purple dress.' His voice was accusing, surprising her by its harshness.

'I prefer this one.'

'It belongs to Rebecca,' he stated. 'I don't like to see you in anything of hers, and particularly not that dress.'

'It's not sexy enough for you, is that it?' she asked sharply. 'You want something that reveals a little more of my body—like the lavender silk?'

'What it looks like has nothing to do with it,' he grated. 'I don't have happy memories of that dress. Rebecca wore it the night she tried to seduce me.'

Libby drew in her breath sharply. She did not want to believe what she was hearing.

'You think I'm making it up?'

'You never told me before that Rebecca...' She found it difficult to go on.

'There are some things a man prefers to forget, and this is one of them,' he told her icily.

Libby recalled the Scotsman also saying her sister had tried the same thing, and her cheeks burned. Even though she was aware of her sister's avarice where men were concerned, it hurt her deeply to hear it at first-hand.

'I'll change,' she whispered, 'but not into the lavender silk. If this dress has unhappy memories for you, then that one has for me.' But what else had she got to wear? She simply had nothing dressy enough for the occasion, absolutely nothing. All of her clothes were either printed or plain cotton. When she was packing they had seemed the perfect thing to wear in a hot country.

'Are you ready yet?' Warwick's voice sounded outside the door and, without waiting for an answer, he walked in. Libby had stripped off the offending dress, and wore only a brief cream satin bra and matching panties, both of which had been a present from her sister the Christmas before last—not the sort of thing she normally bought herself. His eyes flicked mercilessly over her, and Libby felt swift colour scorch her cheeks. Always she promised herself she would bolt her door, and always she forgot.

Damn the man for having the ability to churn her
emotions so violently!

'Having difficulty in deciding?' He glanced swiftly and
disparagingly at the few dresses in her wardrobe. 'Mmm,
there's nothing here; it looks as though it will have to
be the purple dress after all. Where is it?'

Begrudgingly Libby indicated the polythene carrier
pushed in a corner. He frowned harshly as he bent to
retrieve it, plucking out the crumpled dress and holding
it up disbelievingly. 'You did this to it?'

'I told you I never want to wear it again.'

'Well, you're wearing it tonight. Is this really the only
pretty dress you've got?'

'It's the only one I brought with me,' she prevari-
cated. Not for anything would she tell him that she never
went out and so needed nothing special. 'I never realised
I'd be living it up when I came to see Rebecca.'

'Holding a party is hardly living it up. You'd better
press this, Libby, and get it on ultra-quick before my
guests arrive.'

But she knew the skirt would be ruined if she ironed
its myriad tiny pleats. It needed to be professionally
cleaned, or at the very least hung up for several hours.
She said as much to Warwick.

'Then there's only one answer: you need something
new. I won't be long.'

Before she could even open her mouth he had disappeared. Through the window she saw him vault from
the boat and walk sharply towards one of the boutiques
less than a hundred yards away. In minutes he was back,
the dress which he carried over his arm thrust at her with
a terse, 'Get into that quickly.'

It was a most beautiful dress, in a knit similar to the
one she had worn of Rebecca's, and yet nothing like it
at all. In palest aqua, it was lavishly embroidered with
mother-of-pearl sequins. It had very thin straps the same

as her lavender one, which meant she could not wear her bra, and when she pulled it on she looked as though she had been poured into it.

It fitted her perfectly—she was amazed he had known her size—yet it wasn't blatantly sexy. It was elegant, distinctly elegant. She looked even taller, and felt as she had never felt before in her life. Like a princess, like a queen, like a million dollars.

She had blow-dried her hair earlier in an effort to make it look thicker; now she swept it back at one side with a pretty pearl comb of Rebecca's. The dress was sufficiently decorative to need no jewellery, which was just as well because she had nothing that would live up to it, and finally she ventured self-consciously back out into the saloon.

She had heard no one arrive, and was surprised to see Warwick talking to a tall, dark man. They both turned, but it was Warwick's eyes that held hers. Again she was given a thorough examination, and this time his eyes darkened with something that looked like desire. Libby felt her stomach muscles tighten as she moved slowly towards him. She seemed to have no choice; it was as though she was joined to him by an invisible cord which he was relentlessly pulling in.

The other man might not have been there. The air around her was filled with electricity, crackling, tingling through her veins, filling her with both fear and excitement. He took her hands, and the sensations that raced through her were almost more than she could bear. 'I've always known you were beautiful, Libby, but never more so than tonight. You are magnificent.'

'It's a lovely dress, Warwick.'

'It merely adorns natural beauty.'

The powerful chemistry that had drawn her to him in the first place had never been more strong. As her heart clamoured, her mouth grew dry and she touched the tip of her tongue to her lips in an unconsciously provocative gesture.

Warwick's fingers tightened on hers, and for several more seconds, as their eyes held, no one else existed. She felt the effort it took him to let her go, to remember that they were not alone.

'Libby, I'm failing in my duties. This is Ramón Martos, the manager of El Terraplén. Ramón, Libby Eaton.'

'I am very pleased to meet you.' His dark eyes were frankly admiring, his handshake firm. 'I had no idea Warwick had such a glamorous girl living with him. He is indeed a lucky man.'

All these compliments! There was a danger of them going to her head. Beautiful, magnificent, glamorous. And they were speaking about her! Plain Libby Eaton! How had it happened? What had happened? She felt dizzy with the sheer pleasure of men finding her attractive.

'Yes, I am lucky,' agreed Warwick, taking Libby's hand. 'Not only is she beautiful, she is also an excellent cook, and keeps my boat looking like new.'

'I am jealous, Warwick. You have no right keeping her to yourself. Why have you never brought her to El Terraplén?'

'And risk losing her to the likes of you?' laughed Warwick.

It became clear to Libby that Warwick had said nothing to Ramón about her real reason for being here. The dark-skinned man seemed to be under the impression that she was his girlfriend, and who could blame him, the way Warwick had spoken to her just now? Ramón must have found their awareness of each other distinctly embarrassing.

More guests arrived, more introductions were made, and on each occasion Libby was made to feel as though she was someone special. She did not know why Warwick was doing this, and thanked her lucky stars that no one knew he was engaged to Paula. In the circumstances it would have been totally humiliating.

To her delight and pleasure, Maria had been invited. The black-haired woman made her way through the talking throng of people to Libby's side. 'I did not expect to see you again, Libby. Any news of your sister yet?' Maria wore a slinky black dress, and looked truly stunning. No one would guess that she had two grown-up children.

Libby shook her head ruefully. 'I'm afraid not.'

'This is sad, but I also feel sad for Warwick. He will miss you when your holiday's over and you go back to England.'

'He'll miss having someone to cook his meals,' Libby retorted drily. 'That's about all.' And at the moment she had no idea how long her 'holiday' was going to last.

'You're deluding yourself,' smiled Maria knowingly. 'He's scarcely taken his eyes off you all night; I've been watching him.'

'He's just being a gentleman, making sure I'm not feeling left out,' returned Libby drily. Warwick watched her to make sure she did not go off with some other man, that was all. His hold on her was unreasonable and irrational, but there was nothing she could do about it.

Maria smiled. 'I can't believe you're so unaware of what he feels for you.'

'I know exactly what his feelings are,' laughed Libby, hoping she did not sound too false. 'Stop trying to matchmake, Maria.'

'OK, have it your way,' the woman shrugged. 'But I know what I see. That's a beautiful dress you're wearing.'

'Thank you.'

'Is it new?'

Libby nodded.

'Rather an extravagance when you won't be here long. Or was it because of the impact you knew it would have on Warwick?' asked Maria impishly.

'You're impossible!' Libby had no intention of telling her how she had come by the dress. In fact, when she thought of how much it must have cost, and the fact that she felt morally obliged to pay Warwick back, she went hot all over. It would probably take every penny she had left in the bank.

Libby was totally amazed to find herself the centre of attention. Everyone wanted to meet Warwick's new house guest. Never had she had so many men clamouring to talk to her. It was truly a heady feeling. But always she felt Warwick's eyes on her, carefully monitoring her movements, watching with whom she was speaking, how friendly she was with each person.

Her wine glass kept getting refilled by ardent admirers and, unused as she was to drink, Libby felt herself growing distinctly light-headed. Her feet no longer touched the floor, and when Warwick's hand grasped her elbow and he said, 'I think you've had enough to drink, Libby,' she turned to him and giggled.

'Not yet; I'm really enjoying myself. It's a wonderful party!' She raised herself on tiptoe and kissed him full on the mouth. 'Wonderful.'

'You're beginning to remind me of Rebecca,' he muttered harshly. 'Stop now before you make a fool of yourself.'

Stop what? Stop kissing him or stop drinking? Whatever, Libby instantly sobered; there was no way she wanted to be compared to her flirtatious sister. And what right had she to enjoy herself when Rebecca was missing? What was she doing here at all? She ought to be out somewhere looking for her.

At that moment there was a stir as a late-comer stood poised in the doorway, her vivid yellow dress a perfect foil for her glossy black hair.

Paula ensured that everyone noticed her before she made a bee-line for Warwick. Coldly beautiful, her head held haughtily proud on her swan-like neck, she was the cynosure of all eyes. A pathway opened for her like the Red Sea for Moses when he was leading the people to the Promised Land. Her green eyes shot arrows of hatred into Libby's heart.

Libby wished she were a thousand miles away. Warwick had seemed content to let everyone assume she was his girlfriend, and she had done nothing herself to dispute it. Now she was going to look like a fool. Paula would take great pleasure in broadcasting the fact that she was his fiancée and Libby an employee.

She looked up at Warwick, and he saw the anxiety in her eyes. 'Relax, my lovely Libby; Paula's not going to eat you.' But his voice was mocking rather than reassuring.

'My lovely Libby'! He had called her that on her first day here. She had believed it then, but not now, not ever again. She had discovered he was nice to her only when it suited him. As her heart slammed painfully against her ribcage, Libby took a step away, but his hand gripped her arm. 'I promise you, Paula won't create a scene in front of my guests.'

Libby wished she had his confidence. If the malevolent look on Paula's face was anything to go by, the black-haired woman was going to take the greatest pleasure in making mincemeat of her.

CHAPTER SEVEN

'PAULA!' Warwick forestalled anything Paula was going to say, letting go of Libby's arm and holding out his hands. 'I had no idea you were back. How was Madrid? How was the fashion show? Let me get you a drink. You look stunning in that dress.' With ease born of practice, he steered the dark-haired girl through the crowd to the galley where bottles were lined up in rows. Libby had the feeling that she was already forgotten. She had seen how his eyes had lit up, the pleasure he was feeling because his fiancée had put in an unexpected appearance.

Ramón Martos appeared at Libby's side as if by magic, his smile intended to act as a balm, but there was very little that would soothe the pain she was feeling. 'I thought he'd kicked Paula out ages ago,' he muttered, his dark eyes savage on the beautiful girl who had usurped Libby. 'We all know what she's like; she's been hanging around him for years, and always causes trouble if he so much as looks at another girl. Come, let's go up on the deck for some air. It's suddenly very stifling in here.'

Libby did not need asking twice. It was obvious Ramón had no time for Paula. Was his opinion shared by any of the others? She risked a glance around the room, and felt comforted by the sympathetic smiles. They were unbelievably all on her side! Except that none of them knew Warwick and Paula were engaged! How long would it be before the beautiful girl spread the news?

Maria was also outside, and she grimaced compassionately. 'I understood Paula was still in Madrid.

114

Trust her to turn up and spoil the evening. I wonder who told her about the party?'

'It hasn't spoilt it for me,' announced Libby firmly.

The older woman looked at her in disbelief. 'We're none of us fools, Libby. Warwick's been showing you off all night as if you're a prized possession. It's just that Paula's such an old friend he feels he cannot ignore her. A pity, a great pity, don't you agree, Ramón?'

He inclined his head gravely. 'Very much so.'

'Warwick pretends to like me for other people's benefit,' protested Libby vehemently. 'He really has very little time for me.'

'Then why are you living with him?' asked Ramón with a frown. 'It is not the impression I was given.'

'I came out to see my sister, but she's—she's moved without giving me her new address.'

'I do not understand,' said Ramón. 'What has Warwick to do with your sister?'

'Rebecca is Libby's sister,' Maria told him. 'You remember Rebecca?'

Ramón's eyes narrowed as a frown drew his brows together. 'Rebecca is your sister?' he repeated slowly. 'I did not know. I think I now understand why Warwick...' His voice tailed off as he realised he was being indiscreet. 'I am sorry, truly sorry. It is a very difficult situation.'

Maria was looking from one to the other in bewilderment. 'Would you mind telling me what you're talking about?'

It was ironic, thought Libby, that Maria knew she was Rebecca's sister, but not what the girl had done, while Ramón was fully aware of Rebecca's behaviour and yet hadn't known they were related. It made her wonder who else knew among this gathering of people, how many of them were talking behind her back? It was too humiliating by far. All of a sudden it became imperative that she escape.

'Excuse me,' she mumbled and, turning away, she pushed her way back through the crowd towards her cabin. It would be her only refuge until everyone had gone. Head down, she charged forwards, seeing no one, not wanting anyone to see her.

If she had been thinking clearly she would have done no such thing; she would have left the boat altogether and sat in one of the bars or gone walking. Only fate could be so cruel as to position Paula and Warwick right in front of her cabin door. She swung away immediately, but not soon enough.

'Libby, I wondered where you'd got to.' Warwick smiled as if nothing at all was wrong. 'You're not drinking! Please, allow me.'

He moved away from Paula, and busied himself at the improvised bar in the galley. One minute he was telling her she'd had enough to drink, the next he was forcing another one on her, thought Libby furiously. Why didn't he leave her alone?

'I'm so glad I made it in time.' Paula's honey-sweet voice belied the coldness in her eyes. 'I hate missing any of Warwick's glorious parties. He really does know how to entertain.'

Libby muttered something non-committal. She had no wish at all to talk with this girl.

'Of course, I imagine you're quite out of your depth. It was actually very sweet of Warwick to invite you. But he's like that: generous to a fault. It makes no difference to him whether you're an employee or not.'

'I am not his employee!' Libby was stung to retaliate. She'd had about enough of this harsh-faced girl's comments, but nevertheless she still could not bring herself to say that she was Warwick's prisoner. 'I am merely helping him out while I wait for my sister.'

'She won't come back here,' said Paula confidently.

Libby's eyes narrowed. 'Why do you say that?'

'I've heard whispers as to the reason she left. Oh, don't worry, Warwick hasn't told me—he's the soul of discretion; but people talk. I must say I'm surprised at him for letting you stay here; it's——'

Libby deliberately shut her ears to Paula's hurtful words. It was very rare that she got into such a temper that she wanted to hit out, but this girl really aggravated her.

'Here you are, Libby.'

With relief she turned to Warwick and accepted the offered glass, taking a much needed mouthful of what she discovered was nothing but pure tonic water, poured over ice, complete with a slice of lemon.

'Another gin also for you, Paula?'

Libby was grateful for his diplomacy, though wasn't sure whether it was necessary.

Paula shook her head. 'All I want is you back here, darling; I'm missing you.'

She touched his arm and rubbed her body against him, and Libby felt nauseated by this overt display of sexuality. Warwick, though, seemed to be enjoying it, and smiled down at her encouragingly. 'What were you two girls talking about so intently?'

'Rebecca,' said Paula at once, surprising Libby by her frankness. 'Don't you think Libby's wasting her time hanging around when it's quite clear her sister's not going to come back?'

'I'm the one who persuaded Libby to stay,' he told her calmly.

'Persuaded'? thought Libby furiously, wishing now she had told Paula the truth. It was about time she knew what sort of man it was she was going to marry. On the other hand she probably wouldn't even believe it.

Paula's fine brows rose questioningly, then she quickly forced a smile. 'You're a sweet old darling, always looking after the underdog. How much longer is Libby going to wait?'

'For as long as it takes,' Libby interjected coldly, before turning swiftly to mingle back with the crowd. Paula's sweetness was sickening. Surely Warwick could see it was all a sham?

She was not on her own for long, and she chatted and laughed and joked, and to all outward appearances was thoroughly enjoying herself. But in actual fact her mind was far removed from what was going on around her. She could not stop herself from continually glancing across at Warwick and Paula. He was letting the woman monopolise him to the extent that he was ignoring his other guests.

Once he caught Libby looking at him, and she averted her eyes quickly and tried to concentrate on what her companion was saying. Then Maria and Ramón came looking for her, and Maria said there was someone she wished Libby to meet, and would she come back outside?

They led her to a thin young man, very intense, with curly black hair and dark brown eyes. 'This is Antonito, Libby; he is a waiter in Warwick's restaurant at Playa Blanca in Lanzarote. He has something very important to tell you.'

'Si,' the boy nodded. 'My Engleesh, it ees not very good, but I see your—er—your *hermana*. *Comprende usted?*' Libby frowned, shaking her head. 'Rebecca, I think her name.'

'Rebecca?' Libby's eyes widened. 'You've seen my sister? Is that what you're saying?'

He nodded vigorously.

Libby felt her heart try to leap out of her breast. 'Where? When? Have you spoken to her? Oh, my goodness, tell me quickly!'

He looked confused by her rapid succession of words, so Maria spoke to him softly in her native Spanish, and when he answered she translated to Libby, 'He says he saw her two days ago in Playa Blanca. He remembers her because she came to Lanzarote with Warwick once. She was so beautiful that he has never forgotten her.'

'What was she doing in Playa Blanca? Did he speak to her? Did she tell him where she was living?' asked Libby anxiously.

'I don't think so; I think he just happened to see her in the street.'

'I must go there,' said Libby decisively. 'I must find her. This is the first real lead I've had. Was she alone?'

Maria put the question to Antonito and came back with the answer, 'No, she was with a man—a much older man.'

'Did she look happy?'

Antonito shook his head, understanding the question immediately, and went into a torrent of Spanish.

Maria listened and then said quietly, 'He said she looked different, not so sparkling, not so well dressed.'

Libby frowned. The more she heard, the more worried she became. Why was Rebecca neglecting herself? Why, if she had stolen all that money, did she not look beautiful and elegant? And who was the man? Did he have something to do with it? 'This is awful. I really must find her immediately. I'd given up hope that she was still in the Canaries.'

'Of course you must look for her,' agreed Maria softly. 'Until Ramón explained, I had no idea what was really going on. Naturally I wondered why Warwick had asked you to stay with him when you were so insistent there was nothing between you. Now I understand. I'm flying back in the morning, Libby; you can come with me. I will help you search for her. I am sure there has been some huge mistake.'

Libby did not know how she got through the rest of the evening. All she could think about was Rebecca. Warwick had taken second place.

It did not stop her, though, feeling a swift stab of pain when the evening ended and Warwick walked Paula to her waiting taxi. Two heads together, two mouths meeting. She wanted to shut herself in her cabin, she did not want to talk to him again tonight, but she had to tell him about her sister.

When he returned she was collecting glasses and plates and stacking them in the galley ready to be washed. 'Leave those,' he told her brusquely. 'They can be done in the morning.'

'I shan't be here in the morning. I'm going with Maria to Lanzarote.' The words burst out almost defiantly.

'To Lanzarote? With Maria? Whatever for?' He was suddenly tense, his eyes narrowed and watchful.

'Rebecca's been seen there.'

Immediately he became fully alert. 'Why wasn't I told? Who saw her? Where? Where is she now?'

'You think I haven't asked all those questions?' she countered explosively. 'No one knows exactly where she is. Antonito saw her in Playa Blanca. He just happened to mention it to Maria, and naturally she told me.'

'Maria doesn't know why Rebecca left me.'

'She does now,' Libby said. 'Ramón explained.' Warwick swore softly. 'It was no secret, was it?' asked Libby, her tone harsh. 'You told me you had plenty of people on the look-out for her. It seems none of them was as smart as Antonito. And he doesn't even know what she's suspected of.'

'Did he actually speak to her?'

'No, of course not. He's in awe of her, I think—probably half in love with her. He saw her once with you, and thought she was the most beautiful girl in the world. I didn't know you had taken her to Lanzarote?'

'Rebecca came with me wherever I went,' he announced carelessly, 'though normally she stayed on the boat while I conducted my business. I believe there was one occasion when I did take her to the restaurant; it must have been then that Antonito saw her.' He was silent a moment, deep in thought. 'Forget about going with Maria; you'll come with me. If Rebecca's there, I intend to find her.'

Libby had guessed he would insist on going as well, and although she would have preferred to fly, because it was quicker, she knew better than to argue with Warwick.

Sleep eluded Libby that night, and when the sky glimmered its customary gold just before the sun rose over the horizon she was out of bed getting showered and dressed. Even so, Warwick was up before her. She was pleased they were having an early start. All night long she had been unable to get Rebecca out of her mind.

The harbour at Playa Blanca played host to a few fishing vessels and rowing boats and one or two small cruisers, but nothing on the same scale as the *Estoque*. 'What are we going to do?' Libby asked as they left the boat. 'Just walk around in the hope that we shall see Rebecca? Or do you plan to alert the police?'

On the way there he had been silent, deep in thought; now he looked at her sharply. 'No police, no, not at this stage. They haven't proved very satisfactory so far. We'll do this my way.'

'But when we find my sister, what then? Are you still going to press charges?' She hated the thought of Rebecca going to prison.

'Does she deserve anything less?' he snarled.

Libby shuddered at the venom in his voice, and wondered what had happened to the charming man he had been at the party. Prior to Paula arriving he had made her feel so warm and beautiful. Now all he was interested in was finding Rebecca and punishing her. She ought not to have told him; she ought to have gone with Maria and said nothing.

First of all they went to his restaurant on the waterfront, which was a little distance away from the harbour. Warwick sat her at a table shaded by one of the giant blue and white umbrellas while he went inside to talk to Antonito, who had flown back on the same plane as Maria.

Drinking freshly squeezed orange juice, she watched intently every single person who went by: children with their parents, teenagers laughing and playing about, elderly men and women whose pace was more sedate...but there was no Rebecca. Not that she had expected to see her sister straight away; indeed she might no longer be here. In two days she could have moved anywhere. But it was the first real lead Libby had had, and she intended searching every corner.

It really was a pretty place, she thought. What a pity she was here in such harrowing circumstances. The water was a heavenly shade of blue, the sand much paler than in Torviscas. Playa Blanca meant white beach, she understood, and it looked tempting. She would have liked to be down there in her bikini, sunbathing, swimming, snorkelling. She would have liked Warwick to be with her, as a friend, not an enemy, and she wished with all her heart that her sister had not got herself into so much trouble.

It seemed as though she had been out here weeks looking for her, instead of five days. They had been some of the most exciting and disturbing days of her life, and when all this was over she would never forget her time spent in the Canary Islands. But, more than that, she would never forget Warwick Hunter. Whatever happened between them, however he treated her, he would remain a part of her life for ever.

Even in the midst of all her anguish about Rebecca, Libby could not think about him without her heart and pulses racing. He came towards her now, tall and dynamic, looking every inch the successful businessman. His grey mohair trousers moulded the muscularity of his thighs, his white shirt accentuated the deep tan of his skin, and his face was thoughtful.

She looked up at him expectantly. 'Any news?'

'Antonito wasn't the only one who saw her, but only once. No one has seen her again.'

'It seems the wrong people saw her,' she said bitingly, 'not the ones you claim to have asked to keep a lookout. I have a feeling that she may no longer be here.'

'I didn't realise you were a pessimist, Libby. We'll spend a few days doing nothing but keeping our eyes open, questioning people—you still have that photograph you showed me?' She nodded, and searched through her purse until she found it, and handed it to him. 'Sooner or later we'll come up with something, I'm sure. I think now, though, we should go back to the *Estoque*, grab our bathing gear, and make the most of that water out there.'

Libby smiled. 'How did you know that's what I was thinking? I'm so hot it's unbelievable!'

But as she walked back with him to the boat she felt guilty at the pleasure that was forming inside her. Why was it, when she was desperately worried about Rebecca, he could make her feel like this? It was wrong to be doing nothing. They ought to be looking, searching, not enjoying themselves. But even so she hummed to herself as she changed into her black and pink bikini, topping it with pink shorts, and pushing her feet into a pair of white mules. A towel over her arm, a jar of sun-cream in her hand, she joined Warwick on the deck.

He wore nothing but a pair of pale blue swimming shorts, and Libby's heartbeat quickened at the sight of his lean, tanned body. He was watching people and cars disembarking from the Fuerteventura ferry, and she guessed he was looking for Rebecca.

She stood a moment at his side, watching also, but to her disgust feeling more aware of him than the people she was supposedly observing. She wanted to touch her fingers to his dark, hair-roughened skin, she wanted to move closer so that she could inhale his heady muskiness, but more than anything she wanted him to turn and take her into his arms. Her need became an ache and, furious with herself for being so weak, she swung away and stepped off the boat. What had happened to the hatred she'd felt?

Warwick did not move—not until the very last person had got off the ferry; only then did he join her to walk to the beach. 'We must lose no opportunities; every person must be observed. Wherever we go, whatever we're doing, we must remain alert.'

'You don't have to tell me,' snapped Libby. 'It is my sister we're looking for.' She hated the way he was coolly indifferent one moment and passionate the next. She had no such control over her feelings. If he was with her she wanted and needed him—it was as simple as that. Even

Rebecca was almost forgotten. It was no good telling herself she was a fool to feel like this about a man whose interest in her was purely mercenary; she was simply incapable of shutting him out.

Libby enjoyed her swim, but it was nowhere near as exciting as when they'd had a beach to themselves in the moonlight. Even lying on their towels on the sand afterwards, it was impossible to feel any closeness. Warwick was more interested in other people than herself, leaning on his elbows, watching, observing, entirely oblivious to her.

When Libby could stand it no longer she jumped to her feet. 'I'm going back to the boat for a shower.'

'I'll come too.' He rose with lazy ease, and Libby was aware of the admiring glances from a group of teenage girls a few yards away. Little did they know what a swine he really was. She hated herself for feeling like this about him, and hated him for making her do it.

His eyes were still everywhere, darting from person to person, and Libby could have screamed. She was worried about her sister too, and equally anxious to find her, but she wasn't concentrating on her search to the exclusion of all else. He was so intent that he wasn't even talking to her.

Back on board the *Estoque* she lingered over her shower and took her time dressing afterwards. When she finally emerged from her cabin the boat was empty. Where Warwick had gone she had no idea, but if he thought she was going to meekly wait here until he came back he was mistaken. She would go looking for Rebecca too.

The whitewashed houses provided a sparkling backdrop to the sands and the calm seas. There were several new holiday resorts, each with their own swimming pools and open-air bars, tennis courts and

restaurants. Libby wandered through them all, but had
no luck, and when she returned to the *Estoque* it was
dark.

Warwick was back before her. The lights from the boat
streamed like coloured ribbons across the water. She expected him to shout at her for disappearing without
leaving word, but she was ready with her answer. If he
could do it, then so could she.

'Have you had any luck?' he asked the moment she
stepped on board, surprising her by the directness of his
question—and not a word about where she had been!
Obviously now that they were close on the trail to her
sister she was not so important to him.

Libby shook her head, but did not smile.

'It's early days yet,' he replied, his eyes narrowed on
hers. 'Go and get yourself changed; we're eating out.'

If he was going to ignore her the way he had on the
beach, it would be a tension-packed evening—but better
perhaps than eating here. The close confines of the boat
were too much with such an atmosphere between them.

She was not surprised when Warwick took her to his
own restaurant. They sat outside, the coloured umbrellas and tablecloths taking on a softer hue in the
lamplight. Just the other side of the low wall was the
beach where they had lain earlier, and the quiet sea
lapping gently. One or two yachts were tied up, a single
light at the top of each mast. It was a romantic, beautiful
place.

He ordered a jug of sangria, and they nibbled on crisp
bread rolls while waiting for their meal, and all the time
his eyes were on her. No longer was he neglecting her,
no longer was he making her feel hurt and angry.

Libby found it difficult to cope with his swinging
moods. From one minute to the next she did not know
where she stood. She wanted to ignore the softness in

his eyes, the way his fingers stroked the glass as though it were her skin. But—dear lord!—already she was beginning to respond: butterflies were quivering in her stomach, her heart felt as though it were in a race, her palms had grown clammy.

She scooped up her drink and took a long, cooling swallow, then concentrated on picking out the pieces of apple and banana, pear and orange—anything to take her attention away from him. She watched the flickering flames of the candle in its orange bowl, which sheltered it from the faint breeze, and then, unable to help herself, she looked up at him.

He was still watching her, and his hand came down over hers on the table. 'Dear Libby, how worried you look. I'm sure we'll find Rebecca soon.' There was a growling softness to his voice which shivered over the surface of her skin. 'I suggest that just for tonight you try to forget her.'

'The way you seem able to forget Paula?' she snapped, snatching her hand away from his, a spasm of pain crossing her face, angry with herself for responding so easily and so deeply. 'What would she say, do you think, if she knew you were sitting here holding my hand?'

'What I do is my own business,' he replied softly. 'I think perhaps it's time I told you that Paula and I are not engaged; we never have been and never will be. I have no intention at all of marrying her.'

CHAPTER EIGHT

LIBBY'S eyes were as wide as saucers as she looked at
Warwick. 'I don't understand.' Her pulses were ham-
mering, her mouth suddenly dry. 'Paula told me herself.'

He smiled grimly. 'Paula has a habit of making up
stories to suit the occasion.'

'But you didn't contradict her.'

'It was wrong of me,' he admitted. 'It seemed an
amusing thing to do at the time.'

'But now you've decided I ought to be told the truth?
Why?' She could not deny that the news pleased her,
but she could not fathom out why he had gone along
with the lie in the first place.

'Because you deserve the truth.'

Her eyes flashed with sudden contempt. She had done
nothing to deserve it; he was making it up to suit himself.
He was close now to finding Rebecca, and so it didn't
matter any more that he kept up the charade. She would
soon be out of his life for ever. He probably couldn't
wait.

'It didn't look to me last night as though she meant
nothing to you, fiancée or not,' she hissed savagely.
'Once she arrived everyone else was forgotten. We might
as well not have been there. What is it with you—can't
you go a few hours without a woman in your arms?'

'Damn you, Libby,' he snarled, 'that was uncalled
for!'

'The truth hurts, does it?' she flashed back. 'I don't
care what the situation is between you and Paula; just
keep your hands off me. I'm here to look for Rebecca

and nothing else—I'm not after an affair. You seem to have forgotten that I told you I hate your guts.'

'I haven't forgotten.' A muscle jerked dangerously in Warwick's jaw as he spoke. 'But I thought it was something said in the heat of the moment; I didn't like to think that you meant it.'

'Oh, I meant it all right,' she lied, biting her lower lip to stop it quivering.

'And yet you can't stop yourself from responding to me?' He put the question softly, his eyes searching hers for the truth.

Libby swung her head away and looked at the restless ocean curling around rocks and boulders, at a stray dog running across the damp sand and leaving behind a set of footprints. She tried to shut Warwick out of her mind by concentrating on these extraneous objects, but it was impossible, and of its own accord her face turned back to his.

'I don't know why,' she whispered.

'You shouldn't fight it.'

'I don't like being made a fool of. I'm fully aware of the fact that I mean nothing to you, that you are intent only on punishing me for the crime you claim my sister has committed. But you cannot detain me for ever.' Her eyes flashed a vivid purple. 'There has to come a time when you give up.'

'I have every confidence that one day I shall find her. If not here, then she's sure to return home to England. That goes without saying, Libby.'

'Then maybe that's where I should be now.'

His eyes hardened on hers. 'I'll let you go when I'm good and ready. I've lost too much money to give up easily.'

'Is that all you care about?' she snapped. 'Haven't you ever stopped to think that Rebecca might be in some sort of trouble? Who was the man she was with, for instance? And why was she looking like a tramp? Heavens, Warwick, haven't you an ounce of compassion? Does everything have to come down to cold facts?'

The grimness of his jaw should have told Libby to shut up, but she was so angry with him for assuming that he could keep her prisoner for however long he liked, that he could use her and play with her emotions to his heart's content, that she did not care what she said. 'It's about time someone told you that there's more to life than making money and having a good time. There's such a thing as caring about people. Rebecca is in dire trouble, and yet you don't give a damn!'

'Have you quite finished?' There was ice in his eyes now, his face darkly savage in the glow from the candle, all angles and harsh lines.

Libby said nothing; her teeth were clenched, her lips clamped, and beneath the table she had screwed her paper napkin into a ball.

'People do matter to me, Libby. I'm not quite the inhuman monster you're trying to paint. I may not sing your sister's praises, but on the other hand her well-being means more to me than a night's takings.'

Liar! she wanted to shout, but wisely kept silent. She had infuriated Warwick enough. She must not forget that they would be going back to the boat together afterwards, and no matter how much she despised him it was essential that a certain amount of harmony existed between them.

Antonito appeared and set down bowls of steaming soup in front of them, his smile white in the darkness of the night, seeing no trace of the tension that stood between the couple like the raised edge of a blade. 'Enjoy your meal,' he said, still smiling, but Libby could tell that he was nervous because he was serving the owner of the restaurant.

'I think,' said Warwick, 'that we should forget our differences for the time being. There is nothing we can do at the moment to find your sister, so we may as well enjoy ourselves.'

Enjoy themselves? How was that possible? Libby took a deep, steadying breath, but it was several minutes before her fluttering nerves settled, before she was able to calm the fears that had risen up inside her.

The soup was thick and hot and filling, and she wished she had not ordered it. But the grilled sole was excellent, spicy on top with unknown ingredients, and the Canary potatoes, small whole potatoes cooked in their jackets and liberally salted, were a treat she was glad she had not missed.

They kept their conversation to safe topics such as favourite films and books, even their favourite singers, and Warwick surprised her by saying that when he opened his first restaurant he used to sing to entertain the customers.

'But you don't do it any more?' she asked, thinking it was a pity, as she would have liked to hear him. He had a wonderful deep voice.

'I can afford to pay other people now.'

'What sort of songs did you used to sing?' She sat forward, interested, and did not realise that the warmth had come back into her eyes, that she had forgotten her antagonism and was once again feeling the pull of his magnetism.

He smiled softly, his lips quirking. 'Love songs, ballads—romantic songs for romantic evenings.'

'Did you enjoy it?'

Warwick inclined his head. 'The customers did. Music has always been one of the greatest pleasures in my life.'

As well as women, Libby thought, then dismissed it as unworthy. 'Do you play any instruments?'

'The piano and the guitar quite well, but I can get a tune out of almost anything.'

She wanted to ask whether he would sing for her, but was too shy.

'And how about you, little girl with the beautiful name, are you musical?'

She shook her head as memories of the day they had met came back to haunt her. Was it then that she had fallen irrevocably in love with him? Because she was in love with Warwick no matter how many times she told herself that she hated him, no matter how often he angered or hurt or humiliated her. Was it then that, like Cinderella, she had turned into a princess? There had definitely been a transformation. Warwick had made a new woman of her.

'You've drifted away from me.' His eyes were almost navy in the subdued light, and there was a softness in them that seemed to caress her skin.

She shivered faintly as she answered, 'When you said "little girl with the beautiful name", you reminded me of the day we first met. I had no idea that any of this was going to happen.'

'Any of what?' he asked gently.

Libby knew he was waiting for her to mention the awareness that had undeniably built up between them, the strong feelings that were a very real part of their relationship, even though she was prepared to categorically deny them.

Something stronger than life itself drew them inexorably together, and, although his feelings had nothing to do with love and affection—he probably treated many girls the same, Paula being a prime example—Libby knew she would never get over him. He was the first man she had fallen in love with, and it was going to break her heart when the final parting came.

'I didn't know,' she answered slowly, 'that I was going to discover Rebecca had worked for you, or that she had gone missing without a trace along with a sizeable sum of money.' And I definitely had no idea that I was going to fall in love with you, she silently added. 'Nor did I know that you had arranged the whole meeting.'

'Was it that discovery which turned you against me?'

It was what had hurt her, what had made her realise how naïve she was. The first man to make a fuss of her and she had succumbed like a starving child to a crust of bread. She must have been pathetic the way she had allowed him to see how deeply she felt; she had held nothing back, she had let every single feeling flood to the surface. Her cheeks coloured simply thinking about it. And the trouble was, he could do it to her again. A touch, a kiss, a few soft words, and she was putty in his hands.

'Yes, I despised you for that,' she said at length, her tone flat, 'but I also despised myself for not seeing right through you.'

'There was no reason why you should,' he replied. 'I wasn't putting on an act—I really did find you attractive. It wasn't what I'd planned, but——'

'Don't lie to me!' she snapped. 'I don't fit in with your lifestyle at all, so please don't take me for an even bigger fool by suggesting that you prefer me to Paula.' If she hadn't known before, she had known it last night when Paula had turned up at the party. Maybe they weren't engaged, but he thought a lot of her, and Paula definitely had her sights set on him. One day they would get married; Libby was sure of it.

He snorted angrily. 'Why do you twist round everything that I say?'

'Because I know it's the truth,' she snapped.

'You still think I'm using you?'

'Well, aren't you? If I weren't Rebecca's sister you wouldn't have given me a second glance.'

'Why is your opinion of yourself so low?'

She closed her eyes. 'Because I've had it rammed home in the past. Rebecca's the beautiful one, Rebecca's the one who attracted all the boys; I was always left out.'

'And so you made up your mind that you were plain and uninteresting?' he asked sharply. 'You played on it even—made no effort to make yourself more attractive?'

He was so close to the truth that Libby felt like getting up from her chair and running away. Instead she tossed her head haughtily. 'I had my mother to look after; I had no time for going out.'

'All you needed was someone to make you feel good about yourself, to give you a sense of your own worth.' Warwick's tone was softer now.

She wanted to deny it; she did not want him to gloat over the fact that he had had a hand in her metamorphosis, but she nodded nevertheless. 'I do feel different.'

'And do you really think I would have bothered with you if I hadn't felt some sort of an attraction?'

Libby swallowed hard, denying her own feelings, denying everything. 'I still think you did it for Rebecca's sake.'

With a harshly dismissive growl, he scraped back his chair and stood up. 'It's time we went.'

Libby shook her head. 'I'll stay here if you don't mind.' So much for her good intentions of keeping harmony between them!

'I do mind,' he snarled. 'I'm not leaving you here as bait for all the young single men who come along. You do yourself a grave injustice by judging yourself unattractive. Your beautiful hair alone is enough to entice a man to touch it.'

He was behind her now, his hands on the back of her chair ready to draw it away the instant she rose, but as he spoke he stroked her hair, lifting it away from her nape, allowing it to drift through his fingers so that it looked like spun silk in the lamplight. Shivers of sensation slid down Libby's spine, and she wanted to wrest away from him, but it was impossible. As always, she was hypnotised by his touch.

After what seemed interminable minutes he touched her shoulders. 'Get up, Libby, we're going.'

She was a weak-minded fool, she decided, as she obeyed. No matter what he said he was still using her, trying to bind her to him with his sweet talk and soft caresses—until such time as he found Rebecca, and then she would be out of his life for ever!

She wished that she weren't alone on the boat with him; she wished Maria or someone else was staying with them. In this strange place she felt more vulnerable than in Tenerife. Perhaps because there had been a lot more boats and a lot more people milling around at the other resort. The harbour here at Playa Blanca was very quiet and dark at night.

'Don't you think it's too early to go back?' she asked. 'I'd like to go for a walk.' There was still a chance she might see her sister.

'If that's what you want.' But instead of leading her through the village he guided her in the opposite direction along a tiled walkway, which was similar to the one in Tenerife except that there were no restaurants and no lamps. It was quite, quite dark, and when she stumbled his arm came automatically about her shoulders—and stayed there!

'Where does this lead?' she asked, furious to hear the husky tremor in her voice.

'Nowhere in particular. Back out on to the main road eventually.'

From somewhere came the sweet scent of flowers and the rasp of a dozen cicadas. The moon silvered all it touched and the stars in the sky looked like diamonds scattered over a velvet cloth. It was a night for lovers. A tremor shuddered through Libby at the thought.

'Are you cold?'

'Just someone walking over my grave.'

'Nothing to do with the fact that I'm holding you?'

How could he see through her so clearly? Why was it that he always knew what she was thinking and feeling? 'Not a thing,' she said, but too loudly, too firmly. It gave her away.

Although it was too dark for her to see the expression on his face, she felt his fingers tighten on her shoulders. She waited for him to call her a liar, and was relieved when he said nothing, but wished there was some safe topic of conversation so that she could rid her mind of his intoxicating nearness.

'Do you really think we'll find Rebecca here?' she asked him. It wasn't a safe subject—it was probably a highly inflammatory one—but it might serve its purpose.

'If she's still here, yes. It's too small a place for a person to hide. Of course, she might have got wind that I was here, and done another runner.'

'We've only been here a few hours,' insisted Libby. 'She won't have heard yet, surely?'

'She knows my boat.'

'But it's usual for you to pay a visit to your restaurant. We've already been here once, and that didn't frighten her away.'

'Agreed. We'll just have to cross our fingers and pray.'

'We'll spend all day tomorrow looking,' Libby decreed. 'Or at least I will. I'll knock on every door and search every bar and gift shop and supermarket. I've been passive long enough. It's time I did something positive.'

'We'll do it together,' he confirmed.

By now they had reached the road, and Libby tried to twist away from him. 'I can see where I'm walking now.'

His grip tightened and he smiled. 'I like the feel of you against me.'

And, to be truthful, so did Libby. The hard contours of his thighs brushed hers with every step that he took, disturbing and exciting her at the same time. There were other couples strolling along enjoying the balmy night air, all with that special glow that lovers had. If only she were that happy and carefree, thought Libby.

She was still reluctant to go back to the boat, and as they walked through the village she paused to look in a gift-shop window at hand-embroidered tablecloths and fans and beautiful ceramicware, and in a florist's where unusual potted plants were for sale. But finally she could linger no longer; the harbour hove into sight, and so too did the *Estoque*. They were home.

Libby headed straight for her cabin, needing to get away from him as quickly as possible, but she was halted by Warwick's soft words. 'Wait; don't go to bed yet, it's still too early. Let's sit a while outside.'

'I'm tired,' she said tonelessly.

'A minute ago you didn't want to come back; you said it was too early.'

'The walk has worn me out.'

He growled impatiently, disbelievingly. 'If it's my company you don't want, then come out with it.' She remained silent. 'Always afraid of your own feelings, aren't you, Libby?' he taunted. 'There's nothing wrong in feeling sensual, in wanting a man to make love to you. In fact it's the most natural thing in the world when two people who are attracted to each other have been in each other's company for as long as we have.'

Libby lifted her head, shocked by his outspoken words. 'How dare you assume to know what I feel?'

'I don't assume; I know,' he told her bluntly. 'And I think the time has come that we did something about it. I'm tired of backing off every time you get one of your pangs of conscience.'

'You mean you're cold-bloodedly going to set out to seduce me?' she asked in horror, while at the same time her pulses leapt in violent response.

'I mean I think we should relax together and accept whatever happens.'

'It would be wrong to let you make love to me,' she protested. 'It would be all wrong. In fact I have no intention of letting any man make love to me until I'm married.'

'I didn't realise you were so old-fashioned.' There was an amused twist to his mouth as he spoke. 'They're admirable sentiments, but I don't think it's always possible to cling to such beliefs.'

'I intend to,' she told him coldly, fighting the aching need in her stomach that made her want to fling herself into his arms. 'Now, if you'll excuse me, I'm going to bed. Goodnight.'

Before she had even set foot on the steps that led down to the galley and ultimately her cabin, Warwick was behind her, whirling her round to face him. There was no amusement on his face now—nothing but furious anger. 'Dammit, Libby, I will not allow you to do this to me!'

He would not allow it? His words were fuel to the fire that raged inside her. There was a crackle of electricity between them, but before she could give voice to her anger she was rammed against the hardness of his body, her mouth captured in a kiss that sent the blood pounding through her veins.

She fought with every ounce of her strength, kicking and struggling, twisting and turning, but he pinned her arms to her sides and let her get on with it. Her strength was pitiful when compared to his. The kiss went on and on, devouring her senses, eating into her mind, and finally her struggles became weaker and weaker until they ceased altogether.

She did not want to give in—she wanted to fight him for ever; but there were some things over which she had no control, and this was one of them. The worst thing about it all was that he knew how she felt.

With the cessation of her struggles his kiss became less punishing, his lips softening on hers, the tip of his tongue tracing their outline, probing gently until she could fight him no longer, until her lips parted of their own free will and she returned kiss for kiss with an eagerness that would horrify her in her saner moments.

'Can you deny now that you want me to make love to you?' he muttered against her mouth. 'Can you in all honesty deny it, Libby?'

Libby made a noise in the back of her throat that was neither a yes nor a no. A deep, primitive hunger had taken hold of her, and she was afraid of it, afraid to give it free rein, afraid of the consequences, afraid to tell him how she felt.

'I can't hear you, Libby.' His voice was raw, and she knew in that moment that nothing was going to stop the mutual need that was propelling them both forward.

She shook her head raggedly. 'I—I can't deny it.' Her words were breathed into his mouth, still no more than a faint, husky whisper. As always she found it extraordinarily amazing that he had the power to make her forget her shyness, that she felt free of all restraints when locked within the warm circle of his arms. It was almost as though she had known him all her life instead of a few days; she was so in tune with him that whatever he wanted she wanted also. It was a scary feeling.

At her confession she felt a sigh escape him and whisper over the soft flesh of her lips. 'That's what I was hoping you'd say, Libby. I've always known that you wanted me as much as I've wanted you.'

Libby felt a shiver ride over her body, goose-bumps rise up on her skin. At any other time his confidence would have enraged her, but now all she could think about was the spiralling pleasure of his mouth against hers, the thrill of anticipation.

She arched herself into him without conscious thought, her fingertips sliding inside his shirt, exploring hard-packed muscles, feeling the sudden tenseness in him, hearing him groan, feeling his arms tighten until she was welded against the heated, musky maleness of his body.

His fingers touched her nape and slid through the silkiness of her hair at the same time as his mouth explored each curve of her face from her eyebrows and eyelids to her nose and cheekbones, from the pearly lobes of her ears and the fragile skin behind them to the soft, hungry pressure of her mouth.

Libby's nerve-ends triggered into shivering excitement, waves of new and different emotions writhed through her stomach, and her breasts swelled and hardened until she could no longer contain the primitive urge to move her body against his.

Never in her life had she offered herself provocatively to any man, but all of a sudden she was no longer in control of her feelings. She was anxious to be rid of the barriers of clothing that lay between them—she felt like tearing them off so that she could feel Warwick's hard bare body against hers.

Her head fell back as he began a fresh assault on her throat, and her breasts pushed demandingly at him. His tongue rasped, his teeth nipped, and the impatience that she felt running through him mirrored her own feelings. In this one direction they were in complete accord. She wanted to tell him not to take it so slowly, she wanted to beg him to hurry, but no words came, and she let him set the pace.

Almost without her being aware of it, he lifted her up in his arms and carried her through to his state-room. There he expertly undressed her, kissing and stroking each inch of skin as it was exposed, until finally she stood naked in front of him. This time there was no dark night sky to hide her self-consciousness. The electric light was harshly revealing.

But the knowledge that he found her beautiful gave her confidence, and she liked seeing his eyes on her, seeing the hunger in them that made his hands tremble and his eyes glaze with desire.

'I think now it's my turn,' she said daringly and, with a confidence that she had not known she possessed, she undid the buttons on his shirt, touching and kissing his flesh as he had hers, feeling the tenseness in him and the swift indrawn breath. His shoes and his trousers were next, and finally his tight black briefs.

When they came together it seemed the most natural thing in the world, and when he lifted her gently on to the bed her emotions were so overpowering that nothing mattered except this primeval need to be a part of him.

At last his hands cupped her aching breasts, his thumbs stroking her already hardened and sensitised nipples. Warwick knew how she felt, he knew how much she needed him to touch her, and he knew how to draw out of her the ultimate response.

Libby moaned her pleasure, her fingers reaching out instinctively to thread through his hair, to claw the broad-muscled hardness of his back, her body writhing with the sweet agony of sensations she had never known existed.

But even they were multiplied when he took one tender, stimulated nipple into his mouth, brushing it with his tongue and lips, grazing and nipping with his teeth, and finally sucking it so fiercely into his mouth that she felt he was trying to swallow her.

Every inch of her aroused body throbbed and pulsed in harmony, and danced in erotic rhythm as he turned his attention to her other breast. It was as though she had been waiting all her life for this moment of infinite pleasure.

Who would have thought that plain Libby Eaton, whom no man had ever looked at twice, would experience the delights of making love with a man who could have his pick of any girls? She did not doubt that Paula had found her way into his bed on more than one occasion, but she closed her mind to such thoughts, allowing instead the full rush of her emotions to flood every corner of her being.

His mouth moved to the flatness of her stomach, sending quivering darts of pleasure through her as his tongue licked and tasted, making her feel as though hundreds of electric wires were implanted in her, each sending a different shock wave through every one of her nerves.

But it was a one-sided affair. Libby wanted to make love to him too, she wanted him to experience the same mind-shattering sensations. 'Warwick, I——' But words were not needed. Hesitantly at first, and then more boldly as he did not reject her, she touched her hands to his body, feeling the exciting shape of him, touching his nipples as he had hers, putting her tongue to them and tasting the heady maleness of his skin.

She knew by the shuddering movements of his body, by the tensing and jerking of muscles, by the way he called out her name, that she was doing the right things, and it amazed her that she had this knowledge without having been taught. Did making love always come instinctively?

They took it in turns to arouse and stimulate each other's bodies, Libby taking her lead from Warwick, but sometimes knowing intuitively what would please him most. The rough rasp of his hands over her body as her lips caressed him, the harshness of his fingers through her hair, all served to tell her that he was reaching the same heights of desire, and she felt humble that she had so much power.

'Libby——'

She stemmed his words with her mouth over his, revelling in the supreme strength she felt. For once they were equals: they both felt the same pounding heaviness in their groin, they both wanted the other with a desperation born of waiting too long. Now that their flames had been lit there was no putting them out, no holding back. There was no fear inside her now, no worries over the future. Nothing was important except this fundamental need.

'Oh, Libby!' With a groan like that of a man going out of his mind, he rolled on top of her. Her legs parted willingly. One moment he was against her, the next inside her, and Libby arched herself into him, not wanting one inch of space between their bodies. Ignoring the brief spasm of pain that was come and gone before she could even think about it, she felt nothing but the savage, sensual pleasure of his powerful male body.

There was no doubt who was master of the situation now, and she felt herself drowning in a vortex of sensations and feelings so intense, so magic, so wonderful, that she cried out her pleasure, lifting herself to him, reaching out with each successive wave of pleasure that vibrated through her for some as yet unknown pinnacle.

When she thought she could stand the pulsing rhythm no longer, her whole body exploded, and fingers of sweet pain reached out from the hot core of her to every extremity, making her lash and writhe beneath Warwick, clutching his shoulders so tightly that her nails dug in and drew blood.

Within seconds Warwick too was gripped in a spasm of convulsions, and she felt the heat of him inside her and heard her name torn from his lips.

Lying in his arms when it was all over, feeling his sweat-slicked body against hers, Libby knew that she would love this man for all time.

She closed her eyes and drifted into dreamless sleep, knowing nothing until the cabin was filled with harsh morning light. As she moved she felt Warwick's firm, warm body beside her, and memories came flooding back. Oh, God, what had she done? It all seemed so different this morning. How could she have given herself to him so willingly? Whatever had possessed her?

Suppressing a cry of sheer horror, she swung her legs over the edge of the bed, but Warwick's hand gripped her arm before she could get out. 'Where do you think you're going?' he asked in a lazily amused voice.

She turned wide, distressed eyes in his direction. 'I don't know what came over me; I should never have——'

'Libby!' His voice was gently chiding. 'You have no reason for regrets. Come here.'

Reluctantly she let him draw her towards him, and when his arms came about her, when his mouth scorched her skin with a series of tiny kisses, when his hand shaped the soft mounds of her breasts, she was lost again. There was no way she could hold anything back.

He made love to her again, and this time there was none of the fevered urgency that had tempered their actions last night; it was a slow, deliberate, mutual exploration, and the final act was even better. Libby was so moved by it all that she wanted to cry. Where it was all going to end she had no idea, but for the moment she was prepared to accept whatever Warwick had to offer.

They showered afterwards, cramming together in the tiny cubicle, laughing and slipping and then towelling each other dry. This togetherness was a new sensation for Libby. He even came into the galley and helped her get breakfast, though neither of them really felt like eating.

They fed squares of toast to each other and sipped piping hot coffee. Libby's eyes shone with the brilliance of dragonfly's wings, and she was so happy that she thought she would die.

It was not until everything was cleared away that he said he had to go out for a while. 'Lie outside and soak up the sun,' he suggested. 'I shan't be very long.'

'And then we'll go looking for Rebecca?' she pleaded. She felt awful that for the last twelve hours she hadn't given her sister a thought. How was he able to do this to her?

They kissed lingeringly before he went, and Libby's pleasure coiled in her stomach. It really looked as though he had been sincere when he'd said he had no intention of marrying Paula. Although nothing had been said about their future, she felt confident now that he was serious about her. Surely no man could make love to a woman as he had to her and not be serious?

She was so excited that she could not relax. Instead she took a stroll around the harbour, and when Warwick still did not return she wandered through the village, stopping at the *supermercado* to pick up some bread, and drifting into the gift shop to ponder over the intricate needlework.

Outside again, she headed towards Warwick's restaurant. He would surely have finished his business by now. They could walk back to the boat together. What made her look up one of the side-streets, she did not know, but her breath caught in her throat when she saw Warwick in the distance. Not from the sheer excitement of seeing him, but because of the person to whom he was speaking. Even as she watched, the girl disappeared inside one of the houses—and surely it was Rebecca?

CHAPTER NINE

LIBBY'S first instinct was to break into a run, but then she decided she would give Warwick the pleasure of imparting the news. She moved back around the corner, and when he appeared at the bottom of the street she pretended to be walking in his direction.

She waited eagerly for him to tell her that he had found Rebecca, but instead all he did was smile warmly and gather her into his arms. 'You missed me so much you couldn't wait?' he taunted laughingly. 'Well, now you're here why don't we wander down to the restaurant and order a nice cold fruit juice?'

And then he would tell her! Libby happily accompanied him, but when the minutes ticked away and nothing was said, when he acted as though everything was as it had been when he left her an hour or so earlier, she could contain herself no longer. The pleasure died out of her eyes to be replaced by hard, accusing anger.

He saw the difference in her even before she spoke. 'Libby, what is it, what's wrong?'

'What's wrong?' she cried. 'You ask me what's wrong when you've just been talking to my sister and you've told me nothing about it? My God, Warwick, what sort of a man are you?'

'You saw me?' His eyes filled with sadness as he asked the question, but Libby was too uptight to see anything other than the fact that he had deliberately kept the news from her.

'Yes, I saw you all right. I demand that you take me to her right away!'

'Libby,' he said quietly, 'it wasn't your sister. It was someone who looked very much like her. I'm afraid Antonito was mistaken. I'm so sorry after——'

'You're lying!' she yelled. 'I saw her myself. Do you think I wouldn't know my own sister? You wanted to tell the police before you told me; that's it, isn't it? God, what a swine you are, Warwick. I'm going to Rebecca now; I'm going to find out the truth before you put her behind bars.'

She marched away, but he caught her up, gripping her arm so fiercely that it hurt; but Libby felt no pain—except in her heart. Warwick was still playing some sort of game with her. He had probably found out yesterday where Rebecca was, and all the time he had been making love to her the information had been stored away inside his head. And he hadn't told her! And he'd had no plans to tell her!

With hot, savage eyes she glared at him. 'Let me go, you bastard. I'd begun to think that you and I were friends . . . what a fool I've made of myself—yet again.' She tore herself free and began running as fast as she could towards the street where she had seen them talking together. She wasn't sure which house it was, but she would knock on every door until she found Rebecca—and Warwick wasn't going to stop her!

Libby expected every second to hear his feet pounding behind her, to feel his hand on her shoulder again . . . but there was nothing. It seemed he was finally letting her go. She did not look back. She stopped when she thought she was at the house where Warwick had been standing, and knocked on the door. Only then did she glance down the street. It was empty. He had finally accepted that she had the right to speak to her sister. She still could not get over the fact that he hadn't told her. It was so unbelievable.

The door opened and a dark-skinned woman looked at her incomprehensibly when she asked if Rebecca lived there. Libby wished now that she hadn't given Warwick the photograph. What was the word Antonito had used? *Hermana*, that was it. With mime language and the Spanish word for sister, she managed to get the message through, but was acutely disappointed when the woman shook her head.

She tried two more houses before the door was answered by a man aged about forty with dark, greying hair, well-dressed with a handsome face, but close-set, shifty eyes—very shifty eyes. He looked at her suspiciously before she had even uttered a word.

'I am looking for Rebecca Eaton,' she said firmly. 'Have I got the right house?'

She could see that he was ready to shut the door in her face. A movement behind him grabbed her attention, and in the gloom she caught a fleeting glimpse of a shadowy figure. 'Becky!' she squealed, and, taking the man by surprise, she pushed him out of the way and ran into the house.

Only it wasn't Rebecca. It was a girl who looked remarkably like her, with the same corn-coloured hair, the same voluptuous figure, even the same shape face. But there the similarity ended. Her eyes were small and brown, her mouth thin and pinched-looking.

'Oh, I'm sorry,' muttered Libby, backing out of the room. 'I really am sorry. I thought you were my sister. You looked like her from a distance. Forgive me; it was very rude of me to burst in like that. I do apologise.'

Whether they understood a word of what she said,
Libby had no idea. She spun on her heel and shot
through the doorway—into Warwick's arms. But even
the fact that he had been right and she had been wrong
did not alter the way that she felt. It had still been wrong
of him to keep her in the dark. She glared at him angrily,
and ran away down the dusty, narrow street.

Last night and this morning had been such happy occasions, and she really had thought that they would find
Rebecca and so make her happiness complete. Now
everything had gone wrong, and she did not know how
much longer she could live under the same roof as
Warwick. She would never, ever trust him again; she
wanted nothing to do with him. She did not want him
to touch her, or kiss her, or even speak to her.

She wandered down to the water's edge and stood
kicking her toes in the sand. All around were people
laughing and talking, and not one of them knew that
she was the unhappiest girl in the world. She was im-
prisoned here on these islands, with no way of getting
home until Warwick was ready to let her go.

Maybe it was her turn to go to the police. Perhaps she
could tell them that he was holding her on the boat
against her will, and that he had stolen her passport.
But would they believe her? Warwick was a well-known
and respected man. It would be her word against his
and, knowing how ruthless he could be, it was not difficult to work out that he was the one who would end
up on top.

She glanced behind and saw him standing watching
her. With an angry toss of her head, she marched up to
him and almost slapped him across the face when she
saw the humour curling his lips.

'I see nothing funny in the situation,' she snapped.

'Perhaps you'll now learn to believe me.'

Her eyes flashed. 'The way I believed you were going to marry Paula?'

'I didn't actually lie; I let you assume it,' he reminded her.

'It was still a deception, as was keeping to yourself the thought that you had traced Rebecca,' she flung wildly. 'Did you know last night that you could be on her trail?' He nodded briefly. 'So why didn't you tell me?' she demanded, her eyes still hot and fierce. 'How could you have made love to me with that knowledge inside you? No, don't answer; I know. You knew there wasn't a cat in hell's chance that I'd respond to you if I thought I was going to see Rebecca. You're all self, aren't you, Warwick Hunter? Everything to please you; it doesn't matter about me. I'm your prisoner, your property, to be used and abused whenever you feel like it.'

'Libby, stop it.' He looked visibly shaken by her outburst, but when he reached out to her she shrugged angrily away.

'Don't touch me!' she screamed. 'Don't ever touch me again. I hate you. I hate you, Warwick Hunter! I want to go home. I want to go back to England. I want my passport back; you can't keep me prisoner any longer—I won't let you.'

She missed the pain that shadowed his face, heard only the controlled tones of his voice. 'So you've given up your search for Rebecca?'

'Search?' she echoed. 'What searching have I done? You kept telling me everything was under control, that the police and a thousand and one other people were looking for her. And, like a fool, I believed you; I sat back and did nothing—not that I had much choice. I want my passport back, Warwick. If you don't give it to me I shall go to the police and tell them that you've stolen it. See how you like that!'

A muscle jerked in his tightly clenched jaw, and if she had hurt him Libby was glad. But whatever she said or whatever she did it could not possibly hurt him as much as he had hurt her. She wished she had never met him. She wished she had never decided to come out to Tenerife. She wished she knew where Rebecca was. Had her sister any idea how much trouble she was causing?

'I think, Elizabeth, that we should go back to the boat. You might not know it, but we're causing quite a stir.'

Libby looked around her and saw every head turned in their direction, and once again she blamed Warwick. 'It's your fault!' she rasped. 'If my sister had never met you, none of this would have happened. Everything is your fault. Words cannot describe how much I hate you.' She marched resentfully and silently at his side on the short journey to the harbour.

Once on board, with a fan cooling the saloon, which had already grown uncomfortably warm, she turned on him again. 'I'll have my passport and ticket back *now*, Warwick,' she said, holding out her hand. She had no idea how beautiful she looked with two spots of high colour in her cheeks and her violet eyes shining with the brilliance of full-cut diamonds.

'You're in no state to go running off without a clue where you're going,' he told her softly, though there was no accompanying warmth in his eyes. In fact they held no emotion at all. 'If you still want to go home when we get to Tenerife I'll arrange your flight myself.'

He ought to be bitterly ashamed of the way he had handled the situation, thought Libby, though she guessed he wasn't. Men as ruthless as Warwick Hunter didn't possess any feelings. His heart was probably a swinging brick, and last night had been nothing but lust. She realised now that he had lusted after her body from the moment he had met her. He had probably been the same with Rebecca, and that was why she had run away. It served him right if she had stolen his money. He deserved it.

'Maria will look after me,' she told him harshly.

'I don't want Maria involved,' he riposted. 'You're staying on board, Elizabeth, until we reach Tenerife. There is no argument.'

Her angry eyes met his cold indifferent ones, and again she was left wondering how she had ever thought herself in love with him. There was nothing about him to love. He was a man who always put himself first and never cared about anyone else's feelings.

Without another word she flounced through to her cabin, and this time she remembered to bolt the door. But she need not have feared that he would come after her. The engine throbbed into life, and a few minutes later the *Estoque* was nosing her way out of the harbour.

As it was too warm to stay inside, Libby crawled out on to the deck, and in the lee of the cabin, where she was not visible to Warwick on the flybridge, she drew her knees up beneath her chin and stared out at the moody blue of the Atlantic Ocean. So much had happened in such a short space of time. She had never felt so depressed in her life. Her world had been turned upside-down, and she had no idea whether it would ever get back to normal again.

If only Rebecca would turn up; at least then one of her worries would be solved. How could her sister have gone off like this without a word? Unless there was a letter waiting for her at home? Libby could not wait now to get back.

When Warwick called down and asked for a can of Coke, she handed it to him without a word. She never wanted to speak to him again. All the warm, loving feelings had gone, to be replaced with a cold numbness which she guessed would be with her for a long time.

The hours dragged slowly, and it was dark by the time they reached Puerto Colon. The brightly lit marina was a welcome relief with its hustle and bustle, but as Warwick tied up the *Estoque* Libby shut herself back in her cabin.

Seconds later he rapped on the door. 'This is nonsense, Elizabeth; you cannot go on avoiding me. Come out of there at once.' Realising that she was being childish, Libby reluctantly obeyed. 'I don't know about you, but I'm starving,' he said tersely. 'Do you want to eat here or shall we go out?'

'I'm not hungry,' she muttered.

'Neither of us has had anything since breakfast,' he pointed out. 'I realise that you're very angry, but not eating won't help matters.'

'OK, so we'll go out,' she shrugged. It would be infinitely better than sitting here looking at him, hating him, waiting for the moment when she could go home. What a pity it was too late in the day to do anything about changing her ticket.

They went to his own restaurant, Ramón Martos smiling when he saw the two of them together, though his welcome changed to a frown when he saw Warwick's mask-like features and Libby's obvious unhappiness. Tactfully he asked no questions, though Libby saw him looking in their direction several times with a very worried look on his face.

Even though the food was superb, Libby ate very little, unlike Warwick, who finished everything that was put in front of him. It confirmed her opinion that he had no conscience. If he had, how could he eat?

Not until he had sated his appetite did he speak to her. 'Do you know that you're blowing this whole thing up out of all proportion, Elizabeth?' There was still that taut hardness to his jaw and his eyes were as hard as slate. The smoky softness that they'd held on other occasions might have been a figment of her imagination.

'I don't think so,' she replied coldly.

'Why do you think I didn't tell you I thought I was close to finding Rebecca?'

'Because you wanted the police to get at her before me,' she spat savagely.

His mouth grew grim. 'I was hoping you'd said that in the heat of the moment. It's an uncharitable thought.'

'Good!' she cried. 'I'm not feeling very kind towards you at the moment. If that's not the truth, then you tell me why you said nothing.'

He was silent for so long that she thought he wasn't going to answer; then he said quietly, 'I didn't want you getting excited for nothing in case it was a false alarm.'

'And how long has it taken you to think that one up?' she asked frostily. 'I might have believed you if you'd told me earlier, but not now. Oh, no, I've got you weighed up. You don't give a damn about me and my feelings; all you're interested in is number one.'

'That is not true, Elizabeth, and you know it.' The coldness in his eyes matched her own. It was ice that crackled between them now, not electricity, and out of the corner of her eye Libby saw Ramón watching them.

'I know only what I've seen with my own eyes,' she snapped.

'You're prepared to give everything up, everything that has grown between us, because you mistakenly feel that I've let you down? Is that what you're saying?' His frown was harsh, his face angular. 'You won't even admit that you're in the wrong?'

'I am not wrong,' she spat, her voice rising. 'I've never trusted you. Admittedly there have been times when your charm has got through to me, but I realise now how foolish that was. It will never happen again. I want to take the first available flight home. When Rebecca eventually turns up I'll make sure that whatever money she stole—if she did—is returned to you. And I hope that will be an end to it. I don't want to see you ever again.'

A dull red flush suffused Warwick's cheeks, and he pushed his chair roughly back from the table. 'This is hardly the place for such a personal conversation.'

'You started it,' she accused, rising also and glaring at him angrily, entirely heedless of the fact that they were once again attracting attention.

He took her elbow in a grip of iron, and led her forcibly away from the restaurant, only letting her go when they were well clear. Libby hated herself for still feeling an awareness. How could she? It was so pathetic, in the circumstances. What the hell was the matter with her? The instant she was free she moved well away from him, rubbing her arm, feeling sure it would be bruised tomorrow.

Back at the boat, she rushed straight to her cabin and stayed there, throwing herself down on the bed without even undressing. Her thoughts whirled chaotically. Warwick had no idea how important it was to her that she find her sister. Having no brothers or sisters himself, he obviously did not realise how close blood-ties were.

He had no right keeping any information to himself—none at all. He hadn't known it was going to be a false trail. He should have told her. This was what hurt most, and she could not get out of her mind the fact that he had been thinking only of himself, of the money he had lost.

She hated to think what would have happened if it really had been Rebecca, how long it would have been before he told her. She could see now why he hadn't wanted her to fly to Lanzarote with Maria. He had wanted to be in at the kill. God, how she hated him! She couldn't wait to get out of this place. Never again would she return to the Canary Islands. They held nothing but bad memories.

She slept off and on, and woke with a splitting headache and her bad mood in no way diminished. At some stage she had taken off her dress and crawled into bed. Now she threw back the sheets, took a cool shower, and wished that she could magic herself back to England without having to see Warwick Hunter again.

She forced herself to leave her cabin, and when she saw him sitting at the dining table with the coffee-pot in front of him, looking as though yesterday's events had never taken place, she felt like picking up the hot coffee and pouring it over his head. He couldn't possibly look so fresh and clear-eyed if he had a conscience.

Reluctantly she slid on to the opposite seat, pouring herself a drink and swallowing down a couple of aspirin. All without a word being spoken.

But the silence did not last long. 'You're not well?'

It was an abrupt question, asked in a much harsher tone than normal, proving to Libby that although he looked no different he was still in a savage mood. It suited her. This was how she wanted things right up until the time she left.

'I have a headache, that's all,' she answered tersely. 'Is it surprising after what you did to me yesterday?'

'I thought you might have come to your senses.'

Libby looked at him scornfully. 'Have you fixed my flight yet?'

'I phoned through to the airport, but it's bad news. There's nothing until Friday.'

The day after tomorrow? She could not believe it. 'You have to be joking! I can't stay here that long.' There was total horror on her face.

Warwick's lips tightened. 'That's the position, I'm afraid.'

'But surely you can do something? You're wealthy, you're well-known. Can't you fix it?'

'Is it that vital you get away from me?'

'I'm desperate,' she choked.

A muscle jerked in his face. 'Then I suggest you move into the hotel. There is nothing at all I can do to bring your flight forward.'

Libby was not altogether sure that she believed him. He seemed to her to be a very powerful man who could surely pull some strings somewhere. He could probably even afford to charter a private plane to send her back. But no, he didn't want that, did he? He wanted her to suffer some more.

'I'll do it,' she spat. 'Anything will be better than staying here with you. I'll go and pack.'

It took her no time at all to throw her things into her case. She added Rebecca's dresses too, but before she had finished Warwick came into her cabin.

Libby looked up in anger when he pushed open the door. 'Get out!' she screamed. Wasn't he ever going to leave her alone?

'I've telephoned the hotel,' he told her abruptly, his face hard and emotionless. 'They have no vacancies. No one has. You were lucky to get in the last time.'

Libby's eyes flashed. 'You're lying; you're making it up so that you can keep me here and add to my misery.' She was appalled to feel tears pricking the backs of her eyelids, and she turned back to the case, closing the lid and snapping the locks. 'I'll find somewhere. I'll sleep on the beach if I have to—anywhere to get away from you.'

'Damn you, Elizabeth! Damn you and your suspicious mind!' His eyes looked hurt, though she knew that that could not be the case. It was just the way the light was reflecting. 'Stay here, and I'll move out. I'll be back to run you to the airport on Friday. The flight's at eleven.'

'No!' It was an instinctive protest. He looked at her sharply, and waited with raised eyebrows to see what she had to say. 'I—couldn't—I mean—it wouldn't be right to turn you out.'

'It wouldn't be right for you to sleep rough,' he rasped. 'You might not think I'm a gentleman, but that's one thing I would never let you do.'

'Where will you go?' And why was she caring? Why on earth hadn't she let him walk out?

He lifted his wide shoulders. 'Someone will put me up—Ramón, probably.'

'I don't want other people knowing our business.'

'I don't have to tell him.'

Libby grimaced. 'He already knows there's something wrong. He was watching us like a hawk last night.' She sighed and looked at him resignedly. 'You don't have to move out. I'll cope somehow for a couple of days.'

'Forty-eight hours? It's a long time, Elizabeth. Are you sure you can put up with me for that long?'

She ignored the contempt in his tone, and nodded. 'I'll have to, won't I?'

'There's always the Scotsman, of course,' he jeered. 'Haven't you thought about him? I imagine he'd jump at the opportunity of having your delectable presence on board his boat.'

Libby eyed him savagely. 'Your thoughts stink! Get out and stay out. Just keep clear of me.'

Even though the *Estoque* was large in comparison to some other vessels, it was small enough to make Libby feel that she could not move without breathing Warwick in. If only he would shut himself in his office, or go out somewhere—but no, he messed around with the engine, cleaning and checking, he touched up some paintwork, he re-coiled the ropes. He seemed determined to stay close to her.

Libby tried reading her magazine, she tried sun-bathing up on the flybridge, but she could not ignore Warwick. The fact that he was within a few feet of her at all times was sufficient to keep the flames of anger burning, and Libby knew it was going to be an awfully long two days.

She prepared cold meats and tomatoes for their lunch, but ate hers outside while Warwick remained at the dining table. After washing up she climbed off the *Estoque* and, without a word to Warwick, headed in the direction of the footpath to Playa de las Américas. It was the first time she had ever ventured along it, and she was surprised at the number of shops and res-taurants and bars.

She kept going until she was in Américas itself, where she spent another hour or two looking around. What a busy town it was, how many people there were about. A perfect place to remain anonymous. Was Rebecca here? Had she gone no further than this? Every time she saw a blonde head Libby's heartbeats quickened, but it was never her sister.

Eventually she retraced her steps but, avoiding the *Estoque*, she continued to walk around the marina. She did not even think about Iain McTaggart—she was not even looking where she was going, her mind totally absorbed with thoughts of her sister—so when he stepped out in front of her she looked up in total surprise.

'Goodness me, lassie, you were miles away! You look as though you've lost a pound and found a penny. Is something wrong?'

She attempted a smile. 'I was thinking about my sister.'

'You've still not found her, then?'

'I've given up looking,' she confessed. 'I'm going home on Friday. I wanted to go today, but couldn't get a flight.'

'Maybe I can help you there.' Libby frowned and felt her heart flutter. 'I have a friend with a Lear jet. He's always hopping backwards and forwards to Europe. I'm sure he wouldn't mind taking you to England. Would you like me to ask him?'

Would she like him to? Libby almost did a dance on the spot! 'Yes, please!'

'Come on board, and I'll phone him now.'

Without a second thought Libby followed him on to his catamaran, waiting patiently while he telephoned his friend. But again bad luck was with her.

'I'm so sorry,' Iain said. 'According to his secretary, Martin is in Europe at the moment. They're expecting him back on Friday. But that won't be any good to you, will it?' He grimaced ruefully. 'It doesn't look as though this is your lucky day. How about a wee dram to cheer you up?'

Libby shook her head. 'I don't drink.'

'Orange juice? Tea? Coffee? Anything?' he asked with a winning smile.

'I don't think so,' she replied. 'I'd better get back to the *Estoque*. Warwick will be wondering where I am.' Not that she cared, but neither did she wish to stay here.

'He's gone out,' the Scotsman told her. 'I saw him leave in his car over an hour ago.'

'I'll still go,' she said, liking the thought that she would have the boat to herself for a while.

'It doesn't appear to be my lucky day either,' he admitted ruefully. 'Well, if I don't see you again, lassie, have a good flight. I'm certainly going to miss you.'

'You've been very kind.' Libby took his proffered hand, but moved away quickly when she sensed that he was going to kiss her. She could do without complications of that sort. She hurried back to the *Estoque*, expecting to find it empty, and was dismayed beyond measure when Warwick uncurled himself from one of the seats in the saloon. 'Was it worth it?' he barked.

Libby felt bemused by his unexpected attack. 'What are you talking about?'

'I assume you went for consolation? One can only guess what form it took.'

So he had seen her go on to the catamaran, and drawn his own entirely erroneous conclusion! She sighed heavily. 'You really do have a mind like a sewer.'

'Are you denying that you haven't been with that damn Scotsman?' he growled.

'No, I'm not denying it,' she said at once.

He eyed her hardly. 'I don't like to think of you making a fool of yourself.'

'As if I haven't already,' she spat back. 'Don't worry, I know what I'm doing. I have to fill in the hours some way until I get out of here.' Let him make of that what he liked. It was no more than he deserved.

She went down into her cabin and took a shower, then sat on her bed with the towel wrapped around her. When Warwick rapped on her door it could have been a few minutes later or even an hour. She did not know. Time seemed to have lost all meaning.

'I'm going out for a meal, Elizabeth—are you coming?' His tone was sharp and not the least bit inviting.

'No, I'm not hungry.' Which was a lie because she was starving.

'Very well. I won't be late back.'

To her relief he did not try to persuade her, and the moment he had gone she went out to the galley, still swathed in the towel, and made herself a plateful of sandwiches. As soon as it grew dark she went to bed, even though it was really far too early, and when Warwick returned she was asleep.

She awoke in the middle of the night with a raging thirst, but when she saw a chink of light under her door she changed her mind about getting herself a drink. She wanted to steer well clear of Warwick. But he must have heard her moving because his voice came softly from the other side of the door. 'Elizabeth, are you awake?'

Reluctantly she drew back the bolt. 'Yes, I am. I'm thirsty. Was there something that you wanted?'

'I was just checking that you were—all right.'

'Or that I was here!' she retorted in sudden anger, as the truth of the situation hit her. 'Did you think that

I'd nipped across to the catamaran the moment your back was turned? Was that it? I'm sorry if I've disappointed you.'

'Hell, Libby, do we have to argue like this every single time we speak?'

Had the 'Libby' slipped out? she wondered. Was she still 'Libby' in his thoughts, only 'Elizabeth' when he was consciously angry with her? 'How can I be civil when you treat me as you do?'

'Dammit,' he swore explosively, 'I have not harmed a hair on your head! I've given you a roof over your head, and I've tried to help you find your sister. Is this all the thanks I'm going to get?'

'Some help!' she sniffed indelicately, reaching for a glass out of the cabinet and filling it with orange juice. 'If you'll excuse me, I'll go back to my bed. If you wish to mount guard all night, then that's your prerogative. Personally, I'm going back to sleep.'

But sleep had never been further away. How she was going to get through another day and another night, she did not know. 'Damn you, Warwick,' she said out aloud. 'Damn you for doing this to me!'

CHAPTER TEN

To LIBBY'S relief Warwick was nowhere in sight when she got up on Thursday morning. Whether he was deliberately giving her breathing space she was not sure but, whatever, she had never been more thankful in her life.

However, her peace was disrupted when Paula put in an unexpected appearance halfway through the morning. Libby was sitting on the deck sipping fruit juice, enjoying her last hours of this wonderful sunshine, and her smile was less than welcoming when she looked at her visitor.

'Where's Warwick?' Paula asked abruptly. Her elegant, strapless blue sundress showed off her flawless shoulders and perfect tan. She looked cool and poised, and Libby felt more gauche than ever in her dirndl skirt and cotton T-shirt.

'I've no idea.' Libby's tone was frosty. 'He'd gone when I got up. I'll tell him you called.'

Paula looked her over condescendingly. 'You're wasting your time here, you know. You're not Warwick's type at all. How much longer do you intend hanging around?'

Libby's hackles rose. 'As a matter of fact Warwick's not my type either,' she snapped. 'And perhaps it might please you to know that I'm going home tomorrow.'

Paula smiled, though it was the most insincere smile Libby had ever seen. 'That is indeed good news. Without

you to worry about he'll have time to make plans for
our wedding.'

'What wedding?' scorned Libby. This supercilious
woman irritated her beyond measure, and she had a
sudden desire to hit back. 'According to what Warwick
told me, you've made up the whole thing. You're not
engaged, and he has no intention at all of marrying you.'

For several seconds Paula was dumbstruck, her green
eyes staring at Libby in disbelief, then she screamed,
'Warwick wouldn't discuss me with you!'

Libby lifted her shoulders indolently. 'Please yourself
whether you believe me or not; it's the truth.'

Paula suddenly looked ugly; her face flushed, her red
mouth twisted, her eyes were brilliant with hatred.
'You're mistaken, I know you are. I shall come back
and see him when you've gone. You're a vicious little
bitch, making up these lies just because you didn't get
anywhere with him.'

'Oh, I did, believe me.' Libby allowed a cool little
smile. 'Your precious Warwick is quite an expert when
it comes to making love. It's a pity he falls down in other
directions. Actually I can't wait to get out of here. If
you can get him back on your side, you're very welcome
to him.'

Paula's language was enough to turn the air blue. She
flounced off the boat, and Libby knew that their conversation would be relayed back to Warwick at the
earliest opportunity. Not that she cared. Every word she
had spoken was the truth.

The rest of the day was, in comparison, unexciting,
and when Warwick returned it was growing dark. She
had begun to think he wasn't going to come back until
she'd gone to bed, and she would have preferred it that
way. Each time they met was like a confrontation.

'Paula came to see you this morning,' she told him bluntly. She had not intended saying anything about the other girl, but his brooding silence filled the boat with an uncomfortable atmosphere, and it was the first thing that came into her mind.

'Oh, yes?' What had she got to say for herself? was the unspoken question.

'Nothing,' Libby shrugged. 'She just came, that's all.'

'You didn't speak to her?'

'A few words. We passed the time of day. She's coming back after I've gone.'

His thick black brows rose. 'You told her you were going home?' Libby nodded. Swift anger tightened his mouth, but he said nothing more, lapsing once again into introspective silence, completely shutting out Libby.

She could not stay on the boat with him. She picked up her bag and headed for one of the nearby restaurants, where she ordered herself a pizza but only picked at it. She had no way of knowing whether Warwick was pleased or sad that she was leaving. Probably pleased. Otherwise he would surely try to dissuade her. Wouldn't he? He wouldn't have changed her ticket over and made all the arrangements if he hadn't wanted her to go.

When she got back to the boat Warwick was in his cabin—at least she assumed he was because a light shone through a chink in the curtains; but he did not come out to check it was she climbing on board, and within a few minutes she went to bed herself.

This time tomorrow she would be home, she thought. The last eight days had been the longest eight days of her life, and would live in her mind for ever. It was such a short time, and yet so much had happened. She had fallen in and out of love, her sister had gone missing, she had gone through the whole gamut of emotions, and now was left feeling drained and unhappy.

On Friday morning Libby wanted to take a taxi to the airport, but Warwick would not hear of it. 'I'll drive you,' he announced firmly. 'Is your case ready?'

When she nodded he fetched it from her cabin and tucked it away in the boot of his car. Libby resisted the urge to look back as she stepped off the *Estoque* for the last time. Her only memories of this boat were unhappy ones, she told herself firmly.

Sitting beside him was worse than she had expected. Despite the tension that was so thick it could almost be cut with a knife, she could still feel the inevitable magnetism that had drawn her to him in the first place.

She kept her hands firmly clasped together in her lap, and stared unseeingly out of the window. She must not give in to it. He was a dangerous man. If she hadn't been attracted to him, none of this would have happened. She might even have found her sister if she hadn't been so blinded by her love for Warwick that she had wanted to spend every second of her time with him.

It was a tortuous journey, and Libby was glad it was short. He took her case out of the car and insisted on carrying it. He collected her ticket from the appropriate desk and handed it to her together with her passport. He even stood beside her in the queue to check her luggage in.

'I'm sorry it had to end like this, Libby.'

Libby looked at him coldly. 'Sorry? After all the pain you've caused me? Apologies won't make any difference; you're wasting your breath.'

A muscle jerked in his jaw and his eyes became hooded so that it was impossible to read his expression. 'I hope your sister turns up.'

'Why? So that you can have your money back?' she snapped. 'For heaven's sake stop the platitudes; I'm not interested in anything you have to say. I just want to get home and forget all about you.'

Nothing else was said until after her luggage had been weighed and her boarding card handed to her. She had never seen Warwick's jaw so grim, but if he was hurt then it was his own fault. He had treated her abysmally right from the start; only her own innocence had stopped her seeing through him.

She held out her hand in a stiff little gesture. 'Goodbye, Warwick. I'll make sure you get your money back one day.'

'Hell, Elizabeth, the money means nothing to me!' he grated through his teeth.

Her brows rose scornfully. 'I hope you don't expect me to believe that you were interested in finding my sister for any other reason? I've told you before—you haven't an ounce of compassion in you. God help the girl who ever marries you, that's all I can say!'

His expression gave nothing away.

'Incidentally,' she went on, 'I told Paula that you had no intention of ever marrying her. She wasn't very pleased. Actually I don't think she believed me. Maybe you should marry her—you're two for a pair.' With that parting shot she walked away from him, through Passport Control and into the departure lounge. She was safe now; he would be unable to follow her. This really was the end.

Her house in Stepney felt damp and cold and unwelcoming. The first thing Libby did was switch on the central heating, the second thing was to check the mail to see if there were any letters from Rebecca. There was nothing. Up until that moment Libby had not realised how much she had banked on hearing from her sister. In her mind she had been sure there would be some correspondence, even if it was only a postcard.

She put the kettle on and made herself a hot drink, and wondered what her next step should be. All in all Rebecca had only been missing a little over two weeks, which was nothing—not in her sister's eyes, anyway. If she was having a good time somewhere she wouldn't even think about phoning home. Rebecca was very thoughtless in that respect.

It would perhaps be best to wait another week or so and see what happened. If she had still heard nothing then she would go to her local police station and see what course of action they suggested.

Libby was not long in getting back into her normal routine—but how dull it was after the excitement of living with Warwick! No matter how Libby tried she could not stop thinking about him—at first with a great deal of anger and bitterness, but gradually her feeling of betrayal died, leaving only an unutterable sadness. No matter what he had done, no matter how he had treated her, she still loved him. It was a fact of life, and it would never go away.

Her thoughts became filled with the happy times they'd spent together: those first few hours before she had discovered who he really was, skinny-dipping in the moonlight, making love—particularly making love. It had been a truly wonderful experience. There were other little occasions too when she had been happy in his company—though sadly there had been far too many times when they had been at loggerheads.

What was he doing now? she wondered. Had Paula spoken to him? Had she managed to convince him that she was the one he ought to marry? How the thought hurt. Had he found someone else to cook for him and keep his boat clean—or was he doing it himself? Was he happy that she had gone, or was he, like her, tormented by memories?

The days crawled by. One week turned into two. Each time the telephone rang Libby held her breath, wondering if it was Rebecca, or Warwick, but it was never either of them. And then, without any prior warning whatsoever, her sister turned up on the doorstep, a handsome young man in tow. 'Surprise, surprise!' she cried out cheerfully.

Libby was afraid to believe her eyes. 'Becky!' she breathed. 'Thank God you're safe!' And pulled her sister into her arms.

'Of course I'm all right,' said Rebecca. 'Aren't I always?' She turned to the tawny-haired boy. 'This is Chas. Chas, meet my sister, Libby.'

'Hi, Libby, pleased to meet you.' He had an Australian accent, and when Libby took his hand she was surprised by the firmness of his grip. He was about Rebecca's age, tall and muscular, and looked as though he lived most of his life out of doors. He had eyes only for Rebecca.

'You'd better come in,' said Libby, feeling suddenly awkward. 'Have you any idea, Becky, how much trouble you've caused?'

It was Rebecca's turn to look astonished. 'Trouble? What kind of trouble? What are you talking about?'

'Disappearing from Tenerife without a word.'

'That's not true!' defended Rebecca. 'In any case I did try to phone you, but I never got any answer. So I phoned Melanie—you remember Melanie? She said she'd heard you'd gone on holiday to Tenerife. Of course as soon as I heard that I realised you'd find out where I was. A pity you missed me, but I knew Warwick would look after you. Isn't he a fabulous guy? In one way I was sorry to leave, but when Chas asked me to go with him how could I refuse?' She pressed a kiss to the boy's cheek, and his arm came automatically about her shoulders. They were obviously very much in love.

'I'm afraid you've lost me,' said Libby, frowning. 'Why should I have known where you'd gone? Warwick had no idea.'

'But I left a note,' insisted Rebecca. 'I told him that Chas and I were going to work our way around the world. I explained that we had to travel light and that I was forced to leave some of my clothes behind, but that I'd be back one day to pick them up. Didn't he get it? I left it on his bed where I knew he'd be sure to find it.'

Libby's frown deepened. 'According to Warwick there was no note. What about the money? What did you do with that? Have you spent it all? Is that why you've come back home?'

'What money?' It was Rebecca's turn to frown. 'What are you talking about?'

Libby had never doubted her sister's innocence, but it was still a relief to hear it from her own lips, and leaving her clothes was exactly the sort of thoughtless thing she would do. Rebecca would never think that they might be in Warwick's way. 'There was money taken out of Warwick's safe at the same time as you went missing.'

Rebecca's brows slid up, and she quickly put two and two together. 'Meaning,' she said thoughtfully, 'that whoever took the money destroyed my note, knowing full well that I'd get the blame.'

'Do you think it was someone you knew?' asked Libby quickly.

Rebecca shook her head. 'I have no idea. I bet Warwick was really angry, though?'

'You can say that again!' replied Libby. 'He's got all the police in the Canary Islands looking out for you.'

Rebecca shrugged her shoulders, not in the least alarmed. 'Looks as if I've caused a lot of fun.'

'It was no fun, I assure you,' retorted Libby tetchily. 'But now I know you're safe I don't care about it any more. Let me make you both a cup of tea, and how about something to eat? Are you hungry?'

Over their meal Rebecca told Libby that they were working their way through Europe at the moment. 'As we were in France I thought I'd pop over to see you.'

'I'm certainly glad you did,' said Libby. 'How long are you staying?'

But their plans were vague, and Libby was of the opinion that it would not be for very long. Chas, it appeared, could turn his hand to most jobs, and Rebecca just loved going along with him. They actually made a good couple, as they both hated being tied down in one job for very long.

'We're going to see Zelda,' announced Rebecca the next morning.

'I didn't know she was back,' remarked Libby.

'Oh, yes; she didn't stay out there long once Mark lost his job and she had nowhere to live.'

'And how about Mark, what's he doing these days?'

Rebecca shrugged. 'I really have no idea. I've no doubt Zelda will tell me. We'll be back for lunch. Will you be in?'

Libby nodded. 'I have no bookings until five, and then only the one.' Since she'd left England at such short notice a lot of her clients had found someone else to do their hair. It worried her sometimes because she was barely earning enough to make ends meet.

When Rebecca and Chas returned Libby was astonished at the fury on her sister's face. 'What's wrong?' she asked anxiously.

'Can you believe that Mark Sanders? I really thought he was my friend. I'm so angry I could swing for him. What a bastard he is!'

'Becky!' exclaimed Libby, scandalised. 'There's no need for language like that.'

'Wait till you hear what he's done!' cried Rebecca. 'I couldn't believe it when he told me. To think that it was all my fault for inviting him on to the boat in the first place!'

'What are you saying?' asked Libby with a frown and a vague feeling of unease.

'That he's the one. He's the swine who took the money. He actually gloated; can you believe that? He's only back home now because he's spent the whole damn lot!'

Libby shook her head. 'He's confessed?'

Rebecca's breath hissed out angrily. 'When he realised I hadn't been caught, he couldn't help bragging—not only about the money, but other little things as well. I can't believe that he would have let me take the blame. We were so close at one time, before I met Chas.' She grimaced at the blond Australian, then added proudly, 'I bet Mark will be nursing a bruised jaw for a long time. I thought for one moment you were going to kill him!'

'I felt like it,' Chas growled. 'What sort of a guy would let a girl take the blame?'

'We must tell Warwick,' said Rebecca.

But Libby shook her head. 'Please don't; not yet. He might think he needs to apologise to me, and I don't want to see him again.'

'Why ever not?' asked Rebecca, surprised. 'He's such a super guy, how can you possibly not want to see him?'

Libby explained how he had made her his virtual prisoner, omitting only the fact that she had fallen in love with him.

Rebecca was incredulous. 'I can't believe that Warwick would act like that. It doesn't sound like him at all.'

'Well, he did, and I don't want him to know the truth—at least not for a while. I'm not up to facing him again yet.'

Rebecca sighed. 'I think you're making a mistake. You've obviously not seen the side of him that I have. Almost every girl falls in love with Warwick; he's that type of guy.'

'Did you fall in love with him?' asked Chas, his face contorted with jealousy.

Rebecca laughed up into his eyes. 'Of course not. He's far too old for me. Nevertheless he was a most attractive man.' She turned back to Libby. 'If you don't want me to put the record straight, dearest sister, then I won't. You have my word.'

Two days later Rebecca and Chas left to resume their working tour of Europe, and Libby was left feeling more alone than ever. She could not help wondering whether she had done the right thing in making Rebecca promise not to tell Warwick, but what other course was open to her?

It went without saying that he would want to apologise—he was that type of man—and she really could not face the thought of seeing him, or even speaking to him on the telephone. It would hurt far too much. She was quite sure that he had given up all hope of seeing his money again, so why not let sleeping dogs lie? It could do no harm.

Her life went on pretty much as normal. She managed to find a few new customers, but her books were nowhere near as full as they had been before she went to Tenerife. And all the time she thought about Warwick. She loved him so much that it hurt. She had half hoped that she might be having his child, but that hadn't proved to be the case, and she had never felt so miserable in her life.

When, a few weeks later, a complimentary ticket dropped through her letter-box for a hairdressing demonstration by top London stylists, she felt it might be the very thing she needed to cheer her up. She had no idea how or why she had been invited, but it was too good an opportunity to miss. She even made a new dress for the occasion, in a similar shade of mauve to the fateful one she had worn that night Warwick had taken her skinny-dipping, but nowhere near as classy. Although she was an excellent dressmaker Libby always felt that her home-made clothes looked just that—home-made!

Libby took the Tube into central London and then walked the few yards to the hotel where the demonstration was taking place. It was every bit as exciting as she had imagined, and she watched closely how every style was created, watched and learned. There was music and dancing girls as well, and it truly was a spectacular evening, one she would remember for a long, long time.

There was a rush for the door when it was over, and Libby stood to one side, waiting for the crowds to thin. A dark head caught her attention. The man had his back to her on the other side of the room, but she could not help thinking how much like Warwick he looked. It wasn't the first time she had seen someone who reminded her of him, and as on those other occasions her heartbeats quickened.

When he turned she could not believe her eyes. It *was* Warwick! What on earth was he doing at a hair show of all places? She must get out before he saw her too, but it was too late—even as she pushed her way through the stream of people she heard him call out her name.

By the time she reached the door he had caught up with her. A strong hand touched her elbow, and the familiar awareness that she had thought never to feel again surged joyfully through her.

'Libby, are you trying to avoid me?' His wonderful baritone voice said her name with the same inflexion as when they'd first met. 'I know you saw me back there. What's the rush?'

'I have a train to catch,' she said quickly, breathlessly. Oh, goodness, what was he doing to her? Had he any idea at all how her heart was cartwheeling, or her pulses flying? She had thought never to see him again and now here he was, larger than life, looking at her with those well-remembered smoky blue eyes.

'Forget your train, I have a car,' he said gruffly. 'I'll take you myself. We have a lot to talk about.'

'No!' said Libby sharply. 'I—it's late; I just want to go home and go to bed. I'm tired.'

'I'm not letting you catch a train by yourself at this hour, Elizabeth.' A stern tone crept into his voice. 'I'm taking you whether you like it or not.'

Libby knew she had no choice, but she was not happy, and as he walked her to his car in the underground car park she asked sharply, 'What are you doing at a show like this anyway?'

'I wanted to see you.'

Libby frowned and then looked at him suspiciously.
'*You* are responsible for me getting that ticket?' He inclined his head. 'I don't believe this!' she cried in as-
tonishment. 'Why would you want to see me?' And why
had he gone to all this trouble?

'To apologise.'

It suddenly became clear. 'Rebecca's been talking—
when I expressly asked her not to,' she accused angrily.

'Oh, no,' he grinned, 'your sister didn't say a word.
It was her boyfriend who told me the whole story. Chas,
isn't that his name? You can't blame Rebecca for
breaking her promise.'

Trust Rebecca to find some way to let Warwick know
the truth, thought Libby bitterly, and now he was here
and he was awakening all the feelings she had tried not
very successfully to bury. Oh, God, she would need to
be so careful. She had made a fool of herself enough
times already.

'You could have telephoned,' she said sharply. 'You
didn't have to go to all this trouble.'

'It isn't the same thing. Besides, I felt sure you would
refuse to speak to me, or even see me, if I had suggested
a meeting. This way you couldn't get out of it. Here we
are.' He handed her into a maroon Mercedes, and Libby
did not have to tell him the way to her house. At first
it puzzled her, and then she recalled how he'd had her
house watched when he was looking for Rebecca. The
memory made her clamp her lips together in annoyance.

When they stopped outside her house she remained
sitting in the car, hoping he might make his apologies
there. She did not want him inside. It was her haven;
there was nothing there to remind her of him. If he came
in now she would see him for ever sitting in a chair,
standing in the doorway, doing whatever it was he would

do once he was indoors. But he took the key from her fingers and let them both into the house without a word being spoken.

'Would you like a cup of coffee?' she asked coolly. 'I haven't anything stronger.'

'I don't want a drink for the moment, Libby.' His blue eyes were intent on hers. 'Sit down; there's a lot to be said.'

She sat on the edge of the worn sofa, wondering what he thought about her shabby little house. To her it was home, it was clean, and that was all that mattered, but there was none of the luxury to which he was accustomed.

'Are you going to see Mark?' she asked bluntly.

'All in good time, yes,' he answered. 'What concerns me for the moment is that I have done you a terrible injustice.'

'Forget it,' she told him roughly. 'It doesn't matter; it's all water under the bridge.' What a lie that was. His manipulation of her still hurt like hell.

'Oh, but it does matter,' he assured her. 'I treated you despicably, Libby. Ever since Rebecca and Chas came to see me I haven't been able to live with myself.'

It's no more than you deserve, she thought, but aloud said, 'You weren't to know that Rebecca had left a note.'

'I should have realised she would never steal from me. And I shouldn't have tried to make you pay for it. That was a foolish mistake. If there is some way I can make it up to you, Libby, then please let me know.'

'Your apology is enough,' she snapped. 'I'd be happy now if you'd get out of my house.' She kept trying to tell herself that she was glad he was suffering, but deep down inside all she wanted to do was throw herself into his arms. How much she loved this man, and all in vain.

He was here now to put right a wrong, but there was no more to it than that. He had desired her but never loved her. She doubted he was capable of loving any woman. Maria had told her once that he had been engaged and the girl had died. It would appear that it had broken his heart irreparably.

The familiar muscle jerked in his jaw. 'I'd like that cup of coffee you offered me.'

'And then you'll go?' Why was he prolonging the agony?

'If that's what you want.'

To her dismay he followed her, standing in the kitchen doorway watching her movements as she filled the kettle and got out cups. 'How's Iain McTaggart?'

The question took her completely by surprise. Libby had not given Iain a second thought since leaving Tenerife. 'What do you mean, how is he? Why should I know?'

'I thought you were seeing him.' His eyes watched her face carefully.

'Seeing Iain? Why should you think that? As far as I know he's still in Tenerife.'

'Is that the truth, Libby?'

'Of course it's the truth. I've no reason to lie.'

To her amazement his face lightened and he looked as though a weight had been lifted off his shoulders. 'The catamaran's been closed up ever since you flew home. I knew you were pretty close to him, and——'

'You jumped yet again to the wrong conclusion,' Libby finished sharply. 'It seems to be a trait of yours, Warwick.'

He grimaced and nodded. 'What a bastard I am; is it any wonder you hate the sight of me?'

Not any more, she wanted to say, but how could she without giving herself away? It might be better if he went on thinking it.

The kettle boiled and she made the coffee. With the two cups in her hands she tried to walk past him back into the living-room, but he did not move. Instead he took the cups from her and put them down on the work-top. Then, with his hands on her shoulders, his eyes looking deeply into hers, he said, 'Do you think we could start all over again, Libby?'

His question utterly shocked her, and her heart clamoured so violently within her breast that it was painful. 'What—what do you mean?'

'Exactly what I said. We got off to a bad start—well, not exactly, but you know what I mean. Everything went wrong for us. Against my will I found myself attracted to you, and I fought it and fought it and ended up hurting you, the one person I love.'

Libby's mouth fell open. 'You—love—me?' And her heart stopped beating, then began again at double-quick time.

He nodded. 'I know you must find it hard to believe. How could I love you and treat you as I did at the same time? Let's sit down, and I'll try to explain.'

Libby needed no second bidding. Her legs were suddenly too weak to hold her, and when Warwick passed over her coffee her hands shook so badly that the cup rattled in the saucer and she had to put it down.

'It all goes back many years,' he said softly, taking the chair opposite so that he could look at her as he spoke. 'I once loved a girl very, very much. We planned to get married, in fact all the arrangements were made. Then one day I had a phone call from her parents to say that she had died. I couldn't believe it, I refused to believe it. I'd been with her the night before and she'd been perfectly all right. But it was true. She died of a heart attack—we assume the excitement of the wedding was too much for her. Up until then no one had known she had a heart problem. I felt as though half of me had been torn away, as though my whole world had come to an end. It was then that I moved to Tenerife.'

'I'm sorry,' whispered Libby. She had grieved and been upset when her own parents died, but to lose someone as young, someone who was your whole future, was sorrow beyond compare.

'You remind me of her, Libby.'

This was something she had not expected, and her eyes shot wide. 'I do?'

He nodded. 'Not in looks, although she did have blonde hair, but in the things you say and do. Your disposition is so much like Louise's. I guess it's what drew me to you.'

'So why did you—hurt me?' asked Libby hesitantly.

Warwick shook his head in anguish. 'I cannot explain what it was like to find that you were so much like Louise and yet were the sister of the girl who had stolen from me. I thought you might even know about it, be involved in some way. I was angry with myself for feeling attracted to you, and angry with you for being Rebecca's sister. I was determined to make you suffer.'

He had done that all right, thought Libby. So much so that she had come running home to England never wanting to see him again. She'd had no idea at all that he felt this way about her. 'I thought you simply—desired me,' she whispered.

'Oh, lord, no, Libby, far more than that. Letting you go was the hardest thing I've ever had to do, but I knew you needed time to sort yourself out. I'd hurt you badly, and I was aware that if I pushed you too much I could lose you for ever.'

'So you were planning to see me again?'

'Yes, indeed, but perhaps not so soon. Rebecca turning up and explaining about Mark brought everything forward. So now I'm here, and you still hate me—but I want to be given another chance.' He leaned forward and took her hands into his. 'Is there any hope, Libby?'

Her eyes were a soft, misty lavender as they looked into smoky blue. 'There's every hope in the world, Warwick.' Her tone was husky with emotion. 'You see, I don't hate you, I've never truly hated you. I tried to tell myself that I did, but I didn't, I—I love you too.'

It was Warwick's turn to look surprised; he even let go of her hands and sat back in his chair, his mouth open, his eyes incredulous. 'Would you mind saying that again, Libby?'

'I love you,' she said, more firmly this time, accompanying her words with a smile. 'I fell in love with you the first day we met, but——'

'Oh, Libby!' he groaned, and the next second she was pulled into his arms and he held her against him for a very long time. 'Libby, Libby, Libby.'

He looked into her face, at the love shining in her beautiful eyes, at the tremulous smile on her lips, and he kissed her—a kiss that was hunger and pain and joy and relief, a kiss that said it all, a kiss that meant more to Libby than the day he had made love to her.

'If only I'd known, Libby, if only I'd known.'

'Me too,' she whispered shyly. 'I still can't believe that you love someone like me.'

His breath hissed out on a little sigh. 'Rule number one, Libby: when we are married, stop putting yourself down. You're beautiful.'

When we are married? It was like a rosy new dawn; a whole new era in her life was beginning, and she was going to share it with this man whom she loved so very much, whom she had thought was out of her life for ever, who had made her so happy and so sad. In a few short minutes everything had changed yet again. She was beginning to realise that life was like that, that the pattern of it could change dramatically from one minute to the next.

They kissed again, and it was a long time before he lifted his head. She wondered whether he would want her to live on the *Estoque*, or whether they would make their home here in England. It did not matter—nothing mattered as long as she could be with him.

'What's Paula going to say?' she asked. 'Did she ever come back to see you?'

'Oh, yes,' he acknowledged with a smile. 'We had a very interesting conversation. Paula was fun, but she meant nothing to me, and she always knew that. Somehow she sensed the attraction between you and me; that's why she put out the lie that I'd asked her to marry me.'

'So why did you go along with it?' She felt snug and safe in the curve of his arm, and nothing he could tell her about Paula hurt.

His mouth twisted wryly. 'Would you believe to make you jealous? Do you remember when I told you it was all a lie? You were showing your jealousy then, and I thought the time was right. I was trying to force your hand. Unfortunately it backfired. You took great pleasure in reminding me that you hated my guts.'

'Self-defence,' she admitted ruefully.

'And then there was the party. We were getting on so well until Paula turned up. I think I hated her in that moment. She wouldn't let me go, and there was no way I could get back to you. It was a disastrous evening.'

'There were a lot of disasters along the way,' said Libby. 'It's been quite a stormy relationship one way and another.'

He nodded his agreement. 'I should never have made love to you; I should have honoured your principles.'

'So why did you?' she asked, a gentle smile curving her soft mouth.

'To try to convince you that you loved me,' he confessed with a shamefaced grimace.

'I don't think I'd have let you if I didn't,' she whispered. 'Do you know, when I got home I hoped I was having your baby?'

'I've thought about that too,' he admitted. 'That was another reason why I had to see you again. I would have taken care of you even if you didn't love me. I would never have let you struggle to bring up my child alone. I presume you're not pregnant?'

Libby shook her head.

'We'll get married before we—indulge ourselves again,' he told her with a wry smile. 'As soon as possible. I'll get a special licence tomorrow, and I'll ring my parents. They're going to love you, I know. They're for ever asking when I'm going to get married and provide them

Next Month's Romances

Each month you can choose from a world of variety in romance with Mills & Boon. Below are the new titles to look out for next month, why not ask either Mills & Boon Reader Service or your Newsagent to reserve you a copy of the titles you want to buy — just tick the titles you would like to order and either post to Reader Service or take it to any Newsagent and ask them to order your books.

Please save me the following titles:	Please tick	√
DARK RANSOM	Sara Craven	
TAKEN BY STORM	Sandra Field	
LESSON TO LEARN	Penny Jordan	
WALK UPON THE WIND	Patricia Wilson	
WHIRLPOOL	Madeleine Ker	
COERCION TO LOVE	Michelle Reid	
LOVE RULES	Ann Charlton	
HIDDEN MEMORIES	Vanessa Grant	
MAID FOR MARRIAGE	Sue Peters *(Faraway Places)*	
THE SINGING TREE	Anne Weale	
LOVE IS A RISK	Jennifer Taylor	
MIRACLES CAN HAPPEN	Stephanie Howard *(Starsign)*	
BLOSSOMING LOVE	Deborah Davis	
STRONG MAGIC	Christine Greig	
THE STORY PRINCESS	Rebecca Winters	
GOBLIN COURT	Sophie Weston	

If you would like to order these books from Mills & Boon Reader Service please send £1.70 per title to: Mills & Boon Reader Service, P.O. Box 236, Croydon, Surrey, CR9 3RU and quote your Subscriber No:..(If applicable) and complete the name and address details below. Alternatively, these books are available from many local Newsagents including W.H.Smith, J.Menzies, Martins and other paperback stockists from 8th June 1992.

Name:...

Address:...

....Post Code:......................

To Retailer: If you would like to stock M&B books please contact your regular book/magazine wholesaler for details.

You may be mailed with offers from other reputable companies as a result of this application. If you would rather not take advantage of these opportunities please tick box ☐

PENNY JORDAN

A
COLLECTION

From the bestselling author of *Power Play*, *Silver* and *The Hidden Years* comes a special collection of three early novels, beautifully presented in one volume.

Featuring:

SHADOW MARRIAGE
MAN-HATER
PASSIONATE PROTECTION

Available from May 1992   Priced £4.99

Available from Boots, Martins, John Menzies, W.H. Smith, most supermarkets and other paperback stockists.
Also available from Mills & Boon Reader Service, PO Box 236, Thornton Road, Croydon, Surrey CR9 3RU.

W●RLDWIDE

Holiday Romance

Make your holiday extra special with four
new Romances from Mills & Boon.

PLANTATION SUMMER
Angela Devine

VENDETTA BRIDE
Rebecca King

TREACHEROUS PATH
Joanna Neil

A HEART DIVIDED
Lee Stafford

Four Romances by four
popular authors have been
specially chosen for this
exciting gift selection.

What could be easier to pack
for your holiday!

Published: 12th June 1992   Price: £6.80

*Available from Boots, Martins, John Menzies, W.H. Smith,
most supermarkets and other paperback stockists.
Also available from Mills & Boon Reader Service, PO Box 236,
Thornton Road, Croydon, Surrey CR9 3RU.*

AN EXCITING NEW SERIAL BY ONE OF THE WORLD'S BESTSELLING WRITERS OF ROMANCE

BARBARY WHARF is an exciting 6 book mini-series set in the glamorous world of international journalism.

Powerful media tycoon Nick Caspian wants to take control of the Sentinel, an old and well established British newspaper group, but opposing him is equally determined Gina Tyrell, whose loyalty to the Sentinel and all it stands for is absolute.

The drama, passion and heartache that passes between Nick and Gina continues throughout the series - and in addition to this, each novel features a separate romance for you to enjoy.

Read all about Hazel and Piet's dramatic love affair in the first part of this exciting new serial.

BESIEGED

Available soon

Price: £2.99

Available from Boots, Martins, John Menzies, W.H. Smith, most supermarkets and other paperback stockists. Also available from Mills & Boon Reader Service, PO Box 236, Thornton Road, Croydon, Surrey CR9 3RU.

4 FREE
Romances
and 2 FREE gifts just for you!

*You can enjoy all the
heartwarming emotion of true love for FREE!
Discover the heartbreak and the happiness, the emotion
and the tenderness of the modern relationships in
Mills & Boon Romances.*

*We'll send you 4 captivating Romances as a special offer
from Mills & Boon Reader Service, along with the chance to
have 6 Romances delivered to your door each month.*

Claim your FREE books and gifts overleaf...

An irresistible offer from Mills & Boon

Here's a personal invitation from Mills & Boon Reader Service, to become a regular reader of Romances. To welcome you, we'd like you to have 4 books, a CUDDLY TEDDY and a special MYSTERY GIFT absolutely FREE.

Then you could look forward each month to receiving 6 brand new Romances, delivered to your door, postage and packing free! Plus our free newsletter featuring author news, competitions, special offers and much more.

This invitation comes with no strings attached. You may cancel or suspend your subscription at any time, and still keep your free books and gifts.

It's so easy. Send no money now. Simply fill in the coupon below and post it to -
Reader Service, FREEPOST, PO Box 236, Croydon, Surrey CR9 9EL.

NO STAMP REQUIRED

Free Books Coupon

Yes! Please rush me my 4 free Romances and 2 free gifts! Please also reserve me a Reader Service subscription. If I decide to subscribe I can look forward to receiving 6 brand new Romances each month for just £9.60, postage and packing free. If I choose not to subscribe I shall write to you within 10 days - I can keep the books and gifts whatever I decide. I may cancel or suspend my subscription at any time. I am over 18 years of age.

Name Mrs/Miss/Ms/Mr _____ EP18R

Address _____

_____

Postcode_____ Signature _____

Offer expires 31st May 1992. The right is reserved to refuse an application and change the terms of this offer. Readers overseas and in Eire please send for details. Southern Africa write to Book Services International Ltd, P.O. Box 41654, Craighall, Transvaal 2024.
You may be mailed with offers from other reputable companies as a result of this application.
If you would prefer not to share in this opportunity, please tick box. ☐